Eric Mackay, James Fagan

Love Letters of a Violinist

And other Poems

Eric Mackay, James Fagan

Love Letters of a Violinist

And other Poems

ISBN/EAN: 9783337019839

Printed in Europe, USA, Canada, Australia, Japan

Cover: Foto ©Andreas Hilbeck / pixelio.de

More available books at **www.hansebooks.com**

LOVE LETTERS OF A VIOLINIST AND OTHER POEMS. BY ERIC MACKAY

With Illustrations

BY

JAMES FAGAN

New York:

BRENTANO'S

CHICAGO   WASHINGTON   PARIS

TO MARIE

CONTENTS

CONTENTS

I. Ecstasy 215
II. Visions 217
III. The Daisy 218
IV. Probation 219
V. Dante 221
VI. Diffidence 222
VII. Fairies 223
VIII. Spirit Love 225
IX. After Two Days 226
X. Byron 227
XI. Love's Ambition 228
XII. Love's Defeat 230
XIII. A Thunderstorm at Night 231
XIV. In Tuscany 232
XV. A Hero 234
XVI. Remorse 235
XVII. The Mission of the Bard 236
XVIII. Death 237
XIX. To One I Love 239
XX. Ex Tenebra 240
XXI. Victor Hugo 241
XXII. Cynthia 242
XXIII. Philomel 244

x CONTENTS

INTRODUCTORY NOTICE

AT the commencement of the year 1885, a
captivating little volume of poems was
mysteriously issued from the " Leadenhalle
Presse " of Messrs. Field and Tuer—a quaint,
vellum-bound, antique-looking book, tied up on
all sides with strings of golden silk ribbon, and
illustrated throughout with fanciful wood-cuts.
It was entitled " Love Letters by a Violinist,"
and those who were at first attracted by its
title and suggestive outward appearance, un-

tied the ribbons with a certain amount of curi-
osity. Love-letters were surely of a private,
almost sacred character. What "Violinist"
thus ventured to publish his heart-records
openly? and were they worth reading? were
the questions asked by the public, and last,
not least, came the natural inquiry, "*Who
was the 'Violinist'?*" To this no satisfac-
tory answer could be obtained, for nobody
knew. But it was directly proved on perusal
of the book that he was a poet, not a mere
writer of verse. Speculations arose as to his
identity, and Joseph Ellis, the poet, reviewed
the work as follows :—

" Behold a mystery—who shall uncase it?
" A small quarto, anonymous. The publisher
"professes entire ignorance of its origin.
"Wild guesses spring from the mask of a
" 'Violinist '—who can he be? *Unde deriva-
"tur?* A Tyro? The work is too skilful for

"such, though even a Byron. Young? Not
"old. Tennyson? No—he hath not the grace
"of style, at least for these verses. Browning?
"No—he could not unbend so far. Edwin
"Arnold might, possibly, have been equal to
"it, witness, *inter alia*, 'Violetta'; but he is
"unlikely. Lytton Bulwer, a voice from the
"tomb? No. His son, Owen Meredith? A
"random supposition, yet possible. Rossetti
"—again a voice from the tomb? No—he
"wanted the strength of wing. James Thom-
"son, the younger, could have done it, but he
"was too stern. Then, our detective ingenu-
"ity proving incompetent, who? We seek the
"Delphic fane—the oracle replies *Swinburne*.
"Let us bow to the oracular voice, for in
"Swinburne we find all requisites for the work
"—fertility of thought, grace of language, in-
"genuity, skill in the *ars poetica*, wealth of
"words, sensuous nature, classic resources.

" * * * * The writer of the 'Love-Letters' is
" manifestly imbued with the tone and tune of
" Italian poetry, and has the merit of proving
' the English tongue capable of rivalling the
" Italian ' *Canzoni d'Amore.'* * * * * He is a
" master of versification, so is Swinburne—he
" is praiseworthy for freshness of thought,
" novelty, and aptness in imagery, so is Swin-
" burne.   He is remarkable for sustained
" energy, so is Swinburne; and thus it may
" safely be said that, if not the writer of the
" 'Love-Letters,' he deserves to be accredited
" with that mysterious production, until the
" authorship is avowed. * * * * Unto Britan-
" nia, as erst to Italia, has been granted a
" a Petrarch."

Meanwhile other leading voices in the Press
joined the swelling chorus of praise.   *The
Morning Post* took up the theme, and, after
vainly endeavouring to clear up the mystery of

the authorship, went on to say: " The appear-
"ance of this book must be regarded as a
"literary phenomenon. We find ourselves
"lifted at once by the author's genius out of
" the work-a-day world of the England of
" to-day, and transported into an atmosphere as
" rare and ethereal as that in which the poet of
" Vaucluse lived and moved and had his being.
" * * * * In nearly every stanza there are un-
" erring indications of a mind and heart
" steeped in that subtlest of all forms of
" beauty, the mythology of old Greece. The
" reader perceives at once that he has to do
" with a scholar and man of culture, as well
" as with an inspired singer, whose muse need
" not feel abashed in the presence of the high-
" est poets of our own day."

Such expressions as, " A new star of brilliant
" magnitude has risen above the literary hori-
" zon in the anonymous author of the exquisite

" book of ' Love-Letters,' " and " These poems
" are among the most graceful and beautiful
" productions of modern times," became frequent in the best literary journals, and private
opinion concerning the book began to make its
influence felt.   The brilliant writer and astute
critic, George Meredith, wrote to a friend on
the subject as follows:—

" The lines and metre of the poems are easy
" and interthreading and perfectly melodious.
" It is an astonishing production—the work of
" a true musician in our tongue."

The Times' special correspondent, Antonio
Gallenga, expressed himself at some length on
the merits of the " Violinist," and spoke of
him " as one who could conjure up a host of
" noble thoughts and bright fancies, who re-
" joices in a great command of language, with
" a flow of verse and a wealth of rhymes.   It is
" impossible to hear his confessions, to follow

" him in his aspirations, to hear the tale of his
" visions, his trances, his dreams, without
" catching his enthusiasm and bestowing on him
" our sympathy. Each 'Love-Letter' is in
" twenty stanzas—each stanza in six lines.
" The poem is regular and symmetrical as
" Dante's 'Comedy,' with as stately and solemn,
" aye, and as arduous a measure." While the
world of art and letters thus discussed the
volume, reading it meanwhile with such eager-
ness that the whole edition was soon entirely
exhausted, a particularly brilliant and well-
written critique of it appeared in the New York
Independent—a very prominent American jour-
nal, destined afterwards to declare the author's
identity, and to be the first to do so. In the
columns of this paper had been frequently seen
some peculiarly graceful and impassioned
poems, signed by one Eric Mackay—notable
among these being a lyric entitled " The Wak-

ing of the Lark " (included in our present volume), which, to quote the expression of a distinguished New York critic, " sent a thrill
through the heart of America." There are no
skylarks in the New World, but there is a deep
tenderness felt by all Americans for the little

" Priest in grey apparel
" Who doth prepare to sing in air his sinless summer carol,"

and Eric Mackay's exquisite outburst of tender
enthusiasm for the English bird of the morning
evoked from all parts of the States a chorus of
critical delight and approbation. The Rev. T.
T. Munger, of Massachusetts, wrote concerning it:—

" This strikes me as the best poem I have
"seen for a long time. As I read it stanza
"after stanza, with not an imperfect verse, not
"a commonplace, but with a sustained increase
"of pure sentiment and glowing fancy, I was
" inclined to place it beside Shelley's. It is

" not so intellectual as Shelley's, but I am not
"sure that it is not truer. Mackay's is the lark
"itself, Shelley's is himself listening to the lark.
" Besides Shelley makes the lark sing at even-
"ing—as I believe it does—but surely 'it to the
" 'morning doth belong,' and Shakespeare is
" truer in putting it at ' Heaven's gate.' It is a
" great refreshment to us tired workers in the
" prose of life to come across such a poem as
" this, and seldom enough it happens nowadays.
" Tell Mr. Eric Mackay to sing us another
" song."

Paul Hamilton Hayne, an American poet,
praised it in an American paper ; and the cultured Maurice Thompson writes :—" This lark-
" song touches the best mark of simplicity,
"sweetness, and naturalness in its modelling."

This admired lyric was copied from the *Independent* into many other journals, together with
several other poems by the same hand, such as

"A Vision of Beethoven," the beautiful verses addressed to the Spanish violinist, Pablo de Sarasate, and a spirited reply to Algernon Charles Swinburne, reproaching him for the attack which the author of "Tristram of Lyonesse" had made on England's name and fame. One day a simple statement appeared in the *Independent* respecting the much discussed "Love-Letters by a Violinist," that the author was simply a gentleman of good position, the descendant of a distinguished and very ancient family, Eric Mackay, known among his personal friends and intimates as a man of brilliant and extensive learning, whose frequent and long residences abroad have made him somewhat of a foreigner, though by birth an Englishman. A fine linguist, a deep thinker, a profound student of the classics, Mr. Mackay may be ranked among the most cultured and accomplished men of his day, and still

young as he is, will undoubtedly be numbered
with the choice few whose names are destined
to live by the side of poets such as Keats, whom,
as far as careful work, delicate feeling, and
fiery tenderness go, Eric Mackay may be said to
resemble, though there is a greater robustness
and force in his muse, indicative of a strong
mind in an equally strong and healthy body,
which latter advantage the divine Keats had
not, unfortunately for himself and the world.
The innate, hardly restrained vigour of Mr.
Mackay's nature shows itself in such passages
as occur in the sonnets, " Remorse," " A Thunderstorm at Night; also in the wild and terribly
suggestive " Zulalie," while something of hot
wrath and scorn leap out in such lines as those
included in his ode to Swinburne, whom he
addresses :—

" O thou five foot five

"Of flesh and blood and sinew and the rest."

*   *   *   *   *

> " Thou art a bee, a bright, a golden thing
> " With too much honey, and the taste thereof
> " Is sometimes rough, and something of a sting
> " Dwells in the music that we hear thee sing."

*   *   *   *

and

> " Take back thy taunt, I say; and with the same
> " Accept our pardon ; or if this offend,
> " Why, then, no pardon, e'en in England's name.
> " We have our country still, and thou thy fame ! "

At the same time no one in all England does more justice and honor to Swinburne's genius than Eric Mackay.

His own strength as a poet suggests to the reader the idea of a spirited horse reined in tightly and persistently,—a horse which prances wildly at times and frets and foams at the bit, and might, on the least provocation, run wild in a furious and headlong career, sweeping all conventionalities out of its road by a sheer, straight-ahead gallop. Mr. Mackay is,

however, a careful, even precise rider, and he
keeps a firm hand on his restless Pegasus—
so firm that, as his taste always leads him to
depict the most fanciful and fine emotions,
his steady resoluteness of restraint commands
not only our admiration but our respect.
While passionate to an extreme in the " Love-
Letters," he is never indelicate; the coarse,
almost brutal, allusions made by some writers
to certain phases of so-called love, which are
best left unsuggested, never defile the pen of
our present author, who may almost be called
fastidious in such matters.   How beautiful and
all-sufficing to the mind is the line expressing
the utter satisfaction of a victorious lover:—

"Crowned with a kiss and sceptred with a joy!"

No details are needed here—all is said.   The
" Violinist," though by turns regretful, sor-
rowful, and despairing, is supreme throughout.
He speaks of the "lady of his song" as

"The lady for whose sake I shall be strong,

"But never weak or diffident again."

The supremacy of manhood is insisted on always ; and the lover, though he entreats, implores, wonders and raves as all lovers do, never forgets his own dignity. He will take no second-best affection on his lady's part—this he plainly states in verse 19 of Letter V. Again, in the last letter of all, he asserts his mastery— and this is as it should be ; absolute authority, as he knows, is the way to win and to keep a woman's affections. Such lovely fancies as

"Phœbus loosens all his golden hair

"Right down the sky—and daisies turn and stare

"At things we see not with our human wit,"

and

"A tuneful noise

"Broke from the copse where late a breeze was slain,

"And nightingales in ecstacy of pain

"Did break their hearts with singing the old joys,"

abound all through the book. And here it is

as well to mark the decision of our poet, even
in trifles.   The breeze he speaks of is not
hushed, or *still*—none of the usual epithets are
applied to it—it is "*slain*," as utterly and as
pitifully as though it were a murdered child.
This originality of conception is remarkable, and
comes out in such lines as

> " I will unpack my mind of all its fears "—

where the word "*unpack*" is singularly appro-
priate, and again—

> " O sweet To-morrow !   Youngest of the sons
> " Of old King Time, *to whom Creation runs*
> " *As men to God.*"
>   " Where a daisy grows,
> " There grows a joy ! "

and beautiful and dainty to a high degree
is the quaint " Retrospect," where the lover
enthusiastically draws the sun and moon into
his ecstasies, and makes them seem to partake
in his admiration of his lady's loveliness.

A graver and more philosophic turn of mind will be found in "A Song of Servitude," and "A Rhapsody of Death;" but, judged from a critical standpoint, Eric Mackay is a purely passionate poet, straying amongst the most voluptuous imaginings, and sometimes seeming to despise the joys of Heaven itself for the sake of love. Thus he lays himself open to an accusation of blasphemy from ultra-religious persons, yet it must be remembered that in this respect he in no way exceeds the emotions of Romeo and Juliet, Paolo and Francesca da Rimini, or any of those lovers whose passion has earned for their names an undying celebrity.

In closing the present notice we can but express a hope that this volume of Eric Mackay's poems may meet with the welcome it deserves from true lovers of Art; for Art includes Poetry; and Poetry, as properly de-

fined is one of its grandest and most endur-
ing forms.

G. D.

.˙. Some of the miscellaneous poems in this collection (in-
cluding "Beethoven at the Piano") were published by the
author a few years ago, under a pseudonym, now discarded.

LETTER I.

- ——

I.

TEACH me to love thee as a man, in prayer,
　May love the picture of a sainted nun,
　　And I will woo thee, when the day is done,
With tears and vows, and fealty past compare,
And seek the sunlight in thy golden hair,
　　And kiss thy hand to claim thy benison.

II.

I shall not need to gaze upon the skies,
　Or mark the message of the morning breeze,
　　Or heed the notes of birds among the trees,
If, taught by thee to yearn for Paradise,
I may confront thee with adoring eyes
　　And do thee homage on my bended knees.

III.

For I would be thy pilgrim; I would bow
   Low as the grave, and, lingering in the same,
   Live like a spectre; or be burnt in flame
To do thee good.   A kingdom for a vow
I'd freely give to be elected now
   The chief of all the servants of thy fame.

IV.

Yea, like a Roman of the days of old,
   I would, for thee, construct a votive shrine,
   And fan the fire, and consecrate the wine;
And have a statue there, of purest gold,
And bow thereto, unlov'd and unconsoled,
   But proud withal to know the statue thine.

V.

For it were sacrilege to stand erect,
   And face to face, within thy chamber lone,
   To urge again my right to what hath flown:
A bygone trust, a passion coldly check'd!
Were I a king of men, or laurel-deck'd,
   I were not fit to claim thee as mine own.

VI.

What am I then ?   The sexton of a joy,
  So lately slain,—so lately on its bier
  Laid out in state,—I dare not, for the fear
Of this dead thing, regard it as a toy.
It was a splendid Hope without alloy,
  And now, behold! I greet it with a tear.

VII.

It is my pastime, and my penance, too,
  My pride, my comfort, and my discontent,
  To count my sorrows ere the day is spent,
And dream, at night, of love within the blue
Of thy sweet eyes, and tremble through and through,
  And keep my house, as one that doth lament.

VIII.

Have I not sinn'd ? I have; and I am curst,
  And Misery makes the moments, as they fly,
  Harder than stone, and sorrier than a sigh.
Oh, I did wrong thee when I met thee first,
And in my soul a fantasy was nurs'd
  That seem'd an outcome of the upper sky.

IX.

I thought a poor musician might aspire;
   I thought he might obtain from thee a look,
   As Dian's self will smile upon a brook,
And make it glad, though deaf to its desire,
And tinge its ripples with a tender fire,
   And make it thankful in its lonely nook.

X.

I thought to win thee ere the waning days
   Had caught the snow, ere yet a word of mine
   Had pall'd upon thee in the summer shine;
And I was fain to meet thee in the ways
Of wild romance, and cling to thee, and gaze,
   Between two kisses, on thy face divine.

XI.

Aye! on thy face, and on the rippling hair
   That makes a mantle round thee in the night,
   A royal robe, a network of the light,
Which fairies brought for thee, to keep thee fair,
And hide the glories of a beauty rare
   As those of sylphs, whereof the poets write.

XII.

I thought, by token of thy matchless form,
  To curb thy will, and make thee mine indeed,
  From head to foot.   There is no other creed
For men and maids, in safety or in storm,
Than this of love.   Repentance may be warm,
  But love is best, though broken like a reed.

XIII.

" She shall be mine till death ! " I wildly said,
  " Mine, and mine only."   And I vow'd, apace,
  That I would have thee in my dwelling-place;
Yea, like a despot, I would see thee led
Straight to the altar, with a tear unshed,
  A wordless woe imprinted on thy face.

XIV.

I wanted thee.   I yearned for thee afar.
  " She shall be mine," I cried, " and mine alone.
  A Gorgon grief may change me into stone
If I be baulk'd."   I hankered for a star,
And soar'd, in thought, to where the angels are,
  To snatch my prize beyond the torrid zone.

xv.

I heeded not the teaching of the past.
    I heeded not the wisdom of the years.
    "She shall be mine," I urged, "till death appears.
For death, I know, will conquer me at last."
And then I found the sky was overcast;
    And then I felt the bitterness of tears.

xvi.

"Behold!" I thought, "Behold, how fair to see
    Is this white wonder!" And I wish'd thee well
    But, like a demon out of darkest hell,
I marr'd thy peace, and claim'd thee on the plea
Of pride and passion; and there came to me
    The far-off warning of a wedding-bell.

xvii.

A friend of thine was walking to her doom,
    A wife-elect, who, ere the summer sun
    Had plied its course, would weep for what was don,—
A friend of thine and mine, who, in the gloom
Of her own soul, had built herself a tomb,
    To tremble there, when tears had ceas'd to run.

XVIII.

On this I brooded; but ah! not for this
  Did I abandon what I sought the while:
  The dear damnation of thy tender smile,
And all the tortures that were like a bliss,
And all the raptures of a holier kiss
  Than fair Miranda's on the magic isle.

XIX.

I urged my suit. "My bond!" I did exclaim,
  "My pink and white, the hand I love to press,
  The golden hair that crowns her loveliness;
And all the beauties which I cannot name;
All, all are mine, and I will have the same,
  Though she should hate me for my love's excess."

XX.

I knew myself. I knew the withering fate
  That would consume me, if, amid my trust,
  I sued for Hope as beggars for a crust.
"O God!" I cried, entranced though desolate,
"Hallow my love, or turn it into hate."
  And then I bow'd, in anguish, to the dust.

Letter
II
SORROW

LETTER II.

—

I.

YES, I was mad. I know it. I was mad.
    For there is madness in the looks of love;
    And he who frights a tender, brooding dove
Is not more base than I, and not so sad;
For I had kill'd the hope that made me glad,
    And curs'd. in thought, the sunlight from above.

II.

He was a fool, indeed, who lately tried
    To touch the moon, far-shining in the trees,
    He clomb the branches with his hands and knees.
And craned his neck to kiss what he espied.
But down he fell, unseemly in his pride,
    And told his follies to the fitful breeze.

13

III.

I was convicted of as strange a thing,
  And wild as strange; for, in a hope forlorn,
  I fought with Fate.   But now the flag is torn
Which like a herald in the days of spring
I held aloft.   The birds have ceased to sing
  The dear old songs they sang from morn to morn.

IV.

All holy things avoid me.   Breezes pass
  And will not fan my cheek, as once they did.
  The gloaming hies away like one forbid;
And day returns, and shadows on the grass
Fall from the trees; and night and morn amass
  No joys for me this side the coffin-lid.

V.

Absolve me, Sweet !   Absolve me, or I die;
  And give me pardon, if no other boon.
  Aye, give me pardon, and the sun and moon,
And all the stars that wander through the sky
Will be thy sponsors, and the gladden'd cry
  Of one poor heart will thank thee for it soon.

VI.

And mine Amati—my belovèd one—
   The tender sprite who soothes, as best he may,
   My fever'd pulse, and makes a roundelay
Of all my fears—e'en he, when all is done,
Will be thy friend, and yield his place to none
   To wish thee well, and greet thee day by day.

VII.

For he is human, though, to look at him,
   To see his shape, to hear,—as from the throat
   Of some bright angel,—his ecstatic note,
A sinful soul might dream of cherubim.
Aye! and he watches when my senses swim,
   And I can trace the thoughts that o'er him float.

VIII.

Often, indeed, I tell him more than man
   E'er tells to woman in the honied hours
   Of trancèd night, in cities or in bowers;
And more, perchance, than lovers in the span
Of absent letters may, with scheming, plan
   For life's surrender in the fairy towers.

IX.

And he consoles me.　There is none I find,
　None in the world, so venturesome and wild,
　And yet withal, so tender, true, and mild,
As he can be.　And those who think him blind
Are much to blame.　His ways are ever kind;
　And he can plead as softly as a child.

X.

And when he talks to me I feel the touch
　Of some sweet hope, a feeling of content
　Almost akin to what by joy is meant.
And then I brood on this; for Love is such,
It makes us weep to want it overmuch,
　If wayward Fate withhold his full consent.

XI.

Oh, come to me, thou friend of my desire,
　My lov'd Amati!　At a word of thine
　I can be brave, and dash away the brine
From off my cheek, and neutralise the fire
That makes me mad, and use thee as a lyre
　To curb the anguish of this soul of mine.

XII.

Wood as thou art, my treasure, with the strings
  Fair on thy form, as fits thy parentage,
  I cannot deem that in a gilded cage
Thy spirit lives. The bird that in thee sings
Is not a mortal. No! Enthralment flings
  Its charms about thee like a poet's rage.

XIII.

Thou hast no sex; but, in an elfish way,
  Thou dost entwine in one, as in a troth,
  The gleesome thoughts of man and maiden both.
Thy voice is fullest at the flush of day,
But after midnight there is much to say
  In weird remembrance of an April oath.

XIV.

And when the moon is seated on the throne
  Of some white cloud, with her attendants near—
  The wondering stars that hold her name in fear—
Oh! then I know that mine Amati's tone
Is all for me, and that he stands alone,
  First of his tribe, belov'd without a peer.

XV.

Yea, this is so, my Lady! A fair form
  Made of the garner'd relics of a tree,
  In which of old a dryad of the lea
Did live and die.   He flourish'd in a storm,
And learnt to warble when the days were warm
  And learnt at night the secrets of the sea.

XVI.

And now he is all mine, for my caress
  And my strong bow,—an Ariel, as it seems,—
  A something sweeter than the sweetest dreams;
A prison'd wizard that has come to bless
And will not curse, though tortured, more or less,
  By some remembrance that athwart him streams.

XVII.

It is the thought of April.   'Tis the tie
  That made us one; for then the earth was fair
  With all things on't, and summer in the air
Tingled for thee and me.   A soft reply
Came to thy lips, and I was like to die
  To hear thee make such coy confessions there.

XVIII.

It was the dawn of love (or so I thought)
  The tender cooing of thy bosom-bird—
  The beating heart that flutter'd at a word,
And seem'd for me alone to be so fraught
With wants unutter'd! All my being caught
  Glamor thereat, as at a boon conferr'd.

XIX.

And I was lifted, in a minute's space,
  As nigh to Heaven as Heaven is nigh to thee,
  And in thy wistful glances I could see
Something that seem'd a joy, and in thy face
A splendour fit for angels in the place
  Where God has named them all in their degree.

XX.

Ah, none so blest as I, and none so proud,
  In that wild moment when a thrill was sent
  Right through my soul, as if from thee it went
As flame from fire! But this was disallow'd;
And I shall sooner wear a winter shroud
  Than thou revoke my doom of banishment.

Letter
III
REGRETS

LETTER III.

REGRETS.

I.

WHEN I did wake, to-day, a bird of Heaven,
    A wanton, woeless thing, a wandering sprite,
    Did seem to sing a song for my delight;
And, far away, did make its holy steven
Sweeter to hear than lute-strings that are seven;
    And I did weep thereat in my despite.

II.

O glorious sun! I thought, O gracious king,
    Of all this splendour that we call the earth!
    For thee the lark distils his morning mirth,
But who will hear the matins that I sing?
Who will be glad to greet me in the spring,
    Or heed the voice of one so little worth?

III.

Who will accept the thanks I would entone
   For having met thee? and for having seen
   Thy face an instant in the bower serene
Of perfect faith? The splendour was thine own,
The rapture mine; and Doubt was overthrown,
   And Grief forgot the keynote of its threne.

IV.

I rose in haste. I seiz'd, as in a trance,
   My violin, the friend I love the best
   (After thyself, sweet soul!) and wildly press'd,
And firmly drew it, with a master's glance,
Straight to my heart! The sunbeams seem'd to dance
   Athwart the strings, to rob me of my rest.

V.

For then a living thing it did appear,
   And every chord had sympathies for me;
   And something like a lover's lowly plea
Did shake its frame, and something like a tear
Fell on my cheek, to mind me of the year
   When first we met, we two, beside the sea.

VI.

I stood erect, I proudly lifted up
  The Sword of Song, the bow that trembled now,
  As if for joy, my grief to disallow.—
Are there not some who, in the choicest cup,
Imbibe despair, and famish as they sup,
  Sear'd by a solace that was like a vow ?

VII.

Are there not some who weep, and cannot tell
  Why it is thus ?   And others who repeat
  Stories of ice, to cool them in the heat ?
And some who quake for doubts they cannot quell,
And yet are brave ?   And some who smile in Hell
  For thinking of the sin that was so sweet ?

VIII.

I have been one who, in the glow of youth,
  Have liv'd in books, and realised a bliss
  Unfelt by misers, when they count and kiss
Their minted joys; and I have known, in sooth,
The taste of water from the well of Truth,
  And found it good.   But time has alter'd this.

IX.

I have been hated, scorn'd, and thrust away,
　By one who is the Regent of the flowers,
　By one who, in the magic of her powers,
Changes the day to night, the night to day,
And makes a potion of the solar ray
　Which drugs my heart, and deadens it for hours.

X.

I have been taught that Happiness is coy,
　And will not come to all who bend the knee;
　That Faith is like the foam upon the sea,
And Pride a snare, and Pomp a foolish toy,
And Hope a moth whose wings we may destroy;
　And she I love has taught these things to me.

XI.

Yes, thou, my Lady! Thou hast made me feel
　The pangs of that Prometheus who was chain'd
　And would not bow, but evermore maintain'd
A fierce revolt. Have I refused to kneel?
I do it gladly. But to mine appeal
　No answer comes, and none will be ordain'd.

XII.

Why, then, this rancour ? Why so cold a thing
  As thy displeasure, O thou dearest One ?
  I meant no wrong. I stole not from the sun
The fire of Heaven; but I did seek to bring
Glory from thee to me; and in the Spring
  I pray'd the prayer that left me thus undone.

XIII.

I pray'd my prayer. I wove into my song
  Fervour, and joy, and mystery, and the bleak,
  The wan despair that words can never speak.
I pray'd as if my spirit did belong
To some old master, who was wise and strong
  Because he lov'd, and suffer'd, and was weak.

XIV.

I curb'd the notes, convulsive, to a sigh,
  And, when they falter'd most, I made them leap
  Fierce from my bow, as from a summer sleep
A young she-devil. I was fired thereby
To bolder efforts, and a muffled cry
  Came from the strings, as if a saint did weep.

XV.

I changed the theme.   I dallied with the bow
   Just time enough to fit it to a mesh
   Of merry notes, and drew it back afresh
To talk of truth and constancy and woe,
And life, and love, and madness, and the glow
   Of mine own soul which burns into my flesh.

XVI.

It was the Lord of music, it was he
   Who seiz'd my hand.   He forc'd me, as I play'd,
   To think of that ill-fated fairy-glade
Where once we stroll'd at night; and wild and free
My notes did ring; and quickly unto me
   There came the joy that maketh us afraid.

XVII.

Oh! I shall die of tasting in my dreams
   Poison of love and ecstasy of pain;
   For I shall never kneel to thee again,
Or sit in bowers, or wander by the streams
Of golden vales, or of the morning beams
   Construct a wreath to crown thee on the plain!

XVIII.

Yet it were easy, too, to compass this,
   So thou wert kind; and easy to my soul
   Were harder things if I could reach the goal
Of all I crave, and consummate a bliss
In mine own fashion, and compel a kiss
   More fraught with honour than a king's control.

XIX.

It is not much to say that I would die,—
   It is not much to say that I would dare
   Torture, and doom, and death, could I but share
One kiss with thee. For then, without a sigh,
I'd teach thee pity, and be graced thereby,
   Wet with thy tears, and shrouded by thy hair.

XX.

It is not much to say that this is so;
   Yet I would sell my substance and my breath,
   And all the joy that comes from Nazareth,
And all the peace that all the angels know,
To lie with thee, one minute, in the snow
   Of thy white bosom, ere I sank in death!

Letter
IV
YEARNING

LETTER IV.

YEARNINGS.

———

I.

THE earth is glad, I know, when night is spent,
  For then she wakes the birdlings in the bowers;
  And, one by one, the rosy-footed hours
Start for the race; and from his crimson tent
The soldier-sun looks o'er the firmament;
  And all his path is strewn with festal flowers.

II.

But what his mission ?　What the happy quest
  Of all this toil ?　He journeys on his way
  As Cæsar did, unbiass'd by the sway
Of maid or man.　His goal is in the west.
Will he unbuckle there, and, in his rest,
  Dream of the gods who died in Nero's day ?

III.

Will he arraign the traitor in his camp?
  The Winter Comet who, with streaming hair,
  Attack'd the sweetest of the Pleiads fair
And ravish'd her, and left her in the damp
Of dull decay, nor re-illumined the lamp
  That show'd the place she occupied in air.

IV.

No; 'tis not so! He seeks his lady-moon,
  The gentle orb for whom Endymion sigh'd,
  And trusts to find her by the ocean tide,
Or near a forest in the coming June;
For he has lov'd her since she late did swoon
  In that eclipse of which she nearly died.

V.

He knew her then; he knew her in the glow
  Of all her charms. He knew that she was chaste,
  And that she wore a girdle at her waist
Whiter than pearl. And when he eyed her so
He knew that in the final overthrow
  He should prevail, and she should be embraced.

VI.

But were I minded thus, were I the sun,
  And thou the moon, I would not bide so long
  To hear the marvels of thy wedding-song;
For I would have the planets, every one,
Conduct thee home, before the day was done,
  And call thee queen, and crown thee in the throng.

VII.

And, like Apollo, I would flash on thee,
  And rend thy veil, and call thee by the name
  That Daphne lov'd, the loadstar of his fame;
And make myself for thee as white to see
As whitest marble, and as wildly free
  As Leda's lover with his look of flame.

VIII.

And there should then be fêtes that should not cease
  Till I had kiss'd thee, lov'd one! in a trance
  Lasting a life-time, through a life's romance;
And every star should have a mate apiece,
And I would teach them how, in ancient Greece,
  The gods were masters of the maidens' dance.

IX.

I should be bold to act; and thou should'st feel
  Terror and joy combined, in all the span
  Of thy sweet body, ere my fingers ran
From curl to curl, to prompt thee how to kneel;
And then, soul-stricken by thy mute appeal,
  I should be quick to answer like a man.

X.

What! have I sinn'd, dear Lady, have I sinn'd
  To talk so wildly ?   Have I sinn'd in this ?
  An angel's mouth was surely meant to kiss!
Or have I dreamt of courtship out in Inde
In some wild wood ?   My soul is fever-thinn'd,
  And fierce and faint, and frauded of its bliss.

XI.

I will not weep.   I will not in the night
  Weep or lament, or, bending on my knees,
  Appeal for pity!   In the clustered trees
The wind is boasting of its one delight;
And I will boast of mine, in thy despite,
  And say I love thee more than all of these.

XII.

The rose in bloom, the linnet as it sings,
    The fox, the fawn, the cygnet on the mere,
    The dragon-fly that glitters like a spear,—
All these, and more, all these ecstatic things,
Possess their mates; and some arrive on wings,
    And some on webs, to make their meanings clear.

XIII.

Yea, all these things, and more than I can tell,
    More than the most we know of, one and all,
    Do talk of Love.   There is no other call
From wind to wave, from rose to asphodel,
Than Love's alone—the thing we cannot quell,
    Do what we will, from font to funeral.

XIV.

What have I done, I only on the earth,
    That I should wait a century for a word?
    A hundred years, I know, have been deferr'd
Since last we met, and then it was in dearth
Of gladsome peace; for, in a moment's girth,
    My shuddering soul was wounded like a bird.

XV.

I knew thy voice. I knew the veering sound
  Of that sweet oracle which once did tend
  To treat me grandly, as we treat a friend;
And I would know't if darkly underground
I lay as dead, or, down among the drown'd,
  I blindly stared, unvalued to the end.

XVI.

There! take again the kiss I took from thee
  Last night in sleep. I met thee in a dream
  And drew thee closer than a monk may deem
Good for the soul. I know not how it be,
But this I know: if God be good to me
  I shall be raised again to thine esteem.

XVII.

I touched thy neck. I kiss'd it. I was bold.
  And bold am I, to-day, to call to mind
  How, in the night, a murmur not unkind
Broke on mine ear; a something new and old
Quick in thy breath, as when a tale is told
  Of some great hope with madness intertwined.

XVIII.

And round my lips, in joy and yet in fear,
  There seemed to dart the stings of kisses warm.
  These were my honey-bees, and soon would swarm
To choose their queen.   But ere they did appear,
I heard again that murmur in mine ear
  Which seem'd to speak of calm before a storm.

XIX.

"What is it, love?"   I whispered in my sleep,
  And turned to thee, as April unto May.
  "Art mine in truth, mine own, by night and day,
Now and for ever?"   And I heard thee weep,
And then persuade; and then my soul did leap
  Swiftly to thine, in love's ecstatic sway.

XX.

I fondled thee! I drew thee to my heart,
  Well knowing in the dark that joy is dumb.
  And then a cry, a sigh, a sob, did come
Forth from thy lips. . . . I waken'd, with a start,
To find thee gone.   The day had taken part
  Against the total of my blisses' sum.

Letter
V
CONFESSIONS

LETTER V.

CONFESSIONS.

I.

O LADY mine ! O Lady of my Life !
Mine and not mine, a being of the sky
Turn'd into Woman, and I know not why—
Is't well, bethink thee, to maintain a strife
With thy poor servant ? War unto the knife,
  Because I greet thee with a lover's eye ?

II.

Is't well to visit me with thy disdain,
  And rack my soul, because, for love of thee,
  I was too prone to sink upon my knee,
And too intent to make my meaning plain,
And too resolved to make my loss a gain
  To do thee good, by Love's immortal plea ?

43

III.

O friend! forgive me for my dream of bliss.
　Forgive: forget; be just! Wilt not forgive?
　Not though my tears should fall, as through a sieve
The salt sea-sand? What joy hast thou in this:
To be a maid, and marvel at a kiss?
　Say! Must I die, to prove that I can live?

IV.

Shall this be so? E'en this? And all my love
　Wreck'd in an instant? No, a gentle heart
　Beats in thy bosom; and the shades depart
From all fair gardens, and from skies above,
When thou art near. For thou art like a dove,
　And dainty thoughts are with thee where thou art.

V.

Oh! it is like the death of dearest kin,
　To wake and find the fancies of the brain
　Sear'd and confused. We languish in the strain
Of some lost music, and we find within,
Deep in the heart, the record of a sin,
　The thrill thereof, and all the blissful pain.

VI.

For it is deadly sin to love too well,
    And unappeased, unhonour'd, unbesought,
    To feed on dreams; and yet 'tis aptly thought
That all must love. E'en those who most rebel
In Eros' camp have known his master-spell;
    And more shall learn than Eros yet has taught.

VII.

But I am mad to love. I am not wise.
    I am the worst of men to love the best
    Of all sweet women ! An untimely jest,
A thing made up of rhapsodies and sighs,
And unordained on earth, and in the skies,
    And undesired in tumult and in rest.

VIII.

All this is true. I know it. I am he.
    I am that man. I am the hated friend
    Who once received a smile, and sought to mend
His soul with hope. O tyrant! by the plea
Of all thy grace, do thou accept from me
    At least the notes that know not to offend.

IX.

See ! I will strike again the major chord
  Of that great song, which, in his early days,
  Beethoven wrote; and thine shall be the praise,
And thine the frenzy like a soldier's sword
Flashing therein; and thine, O thou adored
  And bright true Lady ! all the poet's lays.

X.

To thee, to thee, the songs of all my joy,
  To thee the songs that wildly seem to bless,
  And those that mind thee of a past caress.
Lo! with a whisper to the Wingèd Boy
Who rules my fate, I will my strength employ
  To make a matin-song of my distress.

XI.

But playing thus, and toying with the notes,
  I half forget the cause I have to weep;
  And, like a reaper in the realms of sleep,
I hear the bird of morning where he floats
High in the welkin, and in fairy boats
  I see the minstrels sail upon the deep.

XII.

In mid-suspension of my leaping bow
   I almost hear the silence of the night;
   And, in my soul, I know the stars are bright
Because they love, and that they nightly glow
To make it clear that there is nought below,
   And nought above, so fair as Love's delight.

XIII.

But shall I touch thy heart by speech alone,
   Without Amati? Shall I prove, by words,
   That hope is meant for men as well as birds;
That I would take a scorpion, or a stone,
In lieu of gold, and sacrifice a throne
   To be the keeper of thy flocks and herds?

XIV.

Ah no, my Lady! though I sang to thee
   With fuller voice than sings the nightingale—
   Fuller and softer in the moonlight pale
Than lays of Keats, or Shelley, or the free
And fire-lipp'd Byron—there would come to me
   No word of thine to thank me for the tale.

XV.

Thou would'st not heed.   Thou would'st not any-when,
  In bower or grove—or in the holy nook
  Which shields thy bed—thou would'st not care to look
For thoughts of mine, though faithful in their ken
As are the minds of England's fighting men
  When they inscribe their names in Honour's book.

XVI.

Thou would'st not care to scan my face, and through
  This face of mine, the soul, for scraps of thought.
  Yet 'tis a face that somewhere has been taught
To smile in tears.   Mine eyes are somewhat blue
And quick to flash (if what I hear be true)
  And dark, at times, as velvet newly wrought.

XVII.

But wilt thou own it ?   Wilt thou in the scroll
  Of my sad life, perceive, as in a hive,
  A thousand happy fancies that contrive
To seek thee out ?   Thy bosom is the goal
Of all my thoughts, and quick to thy control
  They wend their way, elate to be alive.

XVIII.

But there is something I could never bring
　My soul to compass. No ! could I compel
　Thy plighted troth, I would not have thee tell
A lie to God. I'll have no wedding-ring
With loveless hands around my neck to cling;
　For this were worse than all the fires of hell.

XIX.

I would not take thee from a lover's lips,
　Or from the rostrum of a roaring crowd,
　Or from the memory of a husband's shroud,
Or from the goblet where a Cæsar sips.
I would not touch thee with my finger tips,
　But I would die to serve thee.—and be proud.

XX.

And could I enter Heaven, and find therein,
　In all the wide dominions of the air,
　No trace of thee among the natives there,
I would not bide with them—No ! not to win
A seraph's lyre—but I would sin a sin,
　And free my soul, and seek thee otherwhere !

Letter
VI
DESPAIR

LETTER VI.

DESPAIR.

I.

I AM undone. My hopes have beggar'd me,
  For I have lov'd where loving was denied.
  To-day is dark, and Yesterday has died,
And when To-morrow comes, erect and free,
Like some great king, whose tyrant will he be,
  And whose defender in the days of pride?

II.

I am not cold, and yet November bands
  Compress my heart. I know the month is May,
  And that the sun will warm me if I stay.
But who is this? Oh, who is this that stands
Straight in my path, and with his bony hands
  Appeals to me to turn some other way?

53

III.

It is the phantom of my murder'd joy,
　Which once again has come to persecute,
　And tell me tales which late I did refute.
But lo ! I now must heed them, as a boy
Takes up, in tears, the remnants of a toy,
　Or bard forlorn the fragments of a lute.

IV.

It is the ghost that, day by day, did come
　To tempt my spirit to the mountain-peak;
　It is the thing that wept, and would not speak,
And, with a sign, to show that it was dumb,
Did seem to hint at Death that was the sum
　Of all we know, and all we strive to seek.

V.

And now it comes again, and with its eye
　Bloodshot and blear, though pallid in its face,
　Doth point, exacting, to the very place
Where I do keep, that no one may descry,
A lady's glove, a ribbon, and a dry,
　A perjur'd rose, which oft I did embrace.

VI.

It means, perchance, that I must make an end
  Of all these things, and burn them as a fee
  To my Despair, when down upon my knee.
O piteous thing ! have pity; be my friend;
Or say, at least, that blessings will descend
  On her I love, on her if not on me!

VII.

The Shape did smile; and, wildly, with a start,
  Did shrivel up, as when a fire is spent,
  Whereof the smoke obscured the firmament.
And then I knew it had but tried my heart,
To teach me how to play a manly part,
  And strengthen me in all my good intent.

VIII.

And here I stand alone, e'en like a leaf
  In sudden frost, as quiet as the wing
  Of wounded bird, which knows it cannot sing.
A child may moan, but not a mountain chief.
If we be sad, if we possess a grief,
  The grief should be the slave, and not the king.

IX.

Yes, I will pause, and pluck from out the Past
  The full discernment of my sorry cheer,
  And why the sunlight seems no longer clear,
And why, in spite of anguish, and the vast,
The sickly blank that o'er my life is cast,
  I cannot kneel to-day, or shed a tear.

X.

It was thy friendship.   It was this I had,
  This and no more.   I was a fool to doubt,
  I was a fool to strive to put to rout
My many foes:—thy musings tender-glad,
Which all had said:—"Avoid him! he is mad—
  Mad with his love, and Love's erratic shout."

XI.

I should have known,—I should have guess'd in time,—
  That, like a soft mirage at twilight hour,
  My dream would melt, and rob me of its dower.
I should have guess'd that all the heights sublime,
Which look'd like spires and cities built in rhyme,
  Would droop and die, like petals from a flower.

XII.

I should have known, indeed, that to the brave
  All things are servants.   But my lost Delight
  Was like the ship that founders in a night,
And leaves no mark.   How then ?   Is Passion's grave
All that is left beside the sobbing wave ?
  The foam thereof, the saltness, and the blight ?

XIII.

I had a fleet of ships, and where are they ?
  Where are they all ? and where the merchandise
  I treasured once—an empire's golden prize,
The empire of a soul, which, in a day,
Lost all its wealth?   I was deceiv'd, I say,
  For I had reckon'd on propitious skies.

XIV.

I look'd afar, and saw no sign of wrack.
  I look'd anear, and felt the summer breeze
  Warm on my cheek; and forth upon the seas
I sent my ships; and would not have them back,
Though some averr'd a storm was on the track
  Of all I lov'd, and all I own'd of these.

XV.

One ship was " Joy," the second " Truth," the third
   " Love in a Dream," and, last not least of all,
   " Hope," and " Content," and " Pride that hath a Fall."
And they were goodly vessels, by my word,
With sails as strong as pinions of a bird,
   And crew that answer'd well to Duty's call.

XVI.

In one of these—in " Hope "—where I did fly
   A lofty banner,—in that ship I found
   Doom's-day at last, and all my crew were drown'd.
Yes, I was wreck'd in this, and here I lie,
Here on the beach, forlorn and like to die,
   With none to pray for me on holy ground.

XVII.

O sweet my Lady ! If thou pass this way,
   And thou behold me where I lie beset
   By wind and wave, and powerless to forget,
Wilt not approach me thoughtfully and say:—
" This man was true.   He lov'd me night and day
   And though I spurn'd at him, he loves me yet."

XVIII.

Wilt not withhold thy blame, at least to-night,
  And shed for me a tear, as one may grieve
  For people known in books, for men who weave
Ropes out of sand, to lead them to the light?
Oh! treat me thus, and, by thy hand so white,
  I will forego the dreams to which I cleave.

XIX.

Be just to me, and say, when all is o'er,
  When some such book is calmly laid aside:
  "The shadow-men have liv'd and lov'd and died;
The shadow-women will be vexed no more.
But there is One for whom my heart is sore,
  Because he took a shadow for his guide."

XX.

Say only this; but pray for me withal,
  And let a pitying thought possess thee then,
  Whether at home, at sea, or in a glen
In some wild nook. It were a joy to fall
Dead at thy feet, as at a trumpet's call,
  For I should then be peerless among men!

Letter
VII
HOPE

LETTER VII.

HOPE.

I.

O TEARS of mine! Ye start I know not why,
  Unless, indeed, to prove that I am glad,
  Albeit fast wedded to a thought so sad
I scarce can deem that my despair will die,
Or that the sun, careering up the sky,
  Will warm again a world that seem'd so mad.

II.

And yet, who knows? The world is, to the mind,
  Much as we make it; and the things we tend
  Wear, for the nonce, the liveries that we lend.
And some such things are fair, though ill-defined,
And some are scathing, like the wintry wind;
  And some begin, and some will never end.

63

III.

How can I think, ye tears! that I have been
  The thing I was—so doubting, so unfit,
  And so unblest, with brows for ever knit,
And hair unkempt, and face becoming lean
And cold and pale, as if I late had seen
  Medusa's head, and all the scowls of it?

IV.

Oh, why is this?   Oh, why have I so long
  Brooded on grief, and made myself a bane
  To golden fields and all the happy plain
Where once I met the Lady of my Song,
The lady for whose sake I shall be strong,
  But never weak or diffident again?

V.

I was too shorn of hope.   I did employ
  Words like a mourner; and to Her I bow'd,
  As one might kneel to Glory in its shroud.
But I am crown'd to-day, and not so coy—
Crown'd with a kiss, and sceptred with a joy;
  And all the world shall see that I am proud.

VI.

I shall be sated now.   I shall receive
  More than the guerdon of my wildest thought,
  More than the most that ecstasy has taught
To saints in Heaven; and more than poets weave
In madcap verse, to warn us, or deceive;
  And more than Adam knew ere Eve was brought.

VII.

I know the meaning now of all the signs,
  And all the joys I dreamt of in my dreams.
  I realise the comfort of the streams
When they reflect the shadows of the pines.
I know that there is hope for celandines,
  And that a tree is merrier than it seems.

VIII.

I know the mighty hills have much to tell;
  And that they quake, at times, in undertone,
  And talk to stars, because so much alone
And so unlov'd.   I know that, in the dell,
Flowers are betroth'd, and that a wedding-bell
  Rings in the breeze on which a moth has flown.

IX.

I know such things, because to loving hearts
   Nature is keen, and pleasures, long delay'd,
   Quicken the pulse, and turn a truant shade
Into a sprite, equipp'd with all the darts
That once were Cupid's; and the day departs,
   And sun and moon conjoin, as man with maid.

X.

The lover knows how grand a thing is love,
   How grand, how sweet a thing, and how divine
   More than the pouring out of choicest wine;
More than the whiteness of the whitest dove;
More than the glittering of the stars above;
   And such a love, O Love! is thine and mine.

XI.

To me the world, to-day, has grown so fair
   I dare not trust myself to think of it.
   Visions of light around me seem to flit,
And Phœbus loosens all his golden hair
Right down the sky; and daisies turn and stare
   At things we see not with our human wit.

XII.

And here, beside me, there are mosses green
  In shelter'd nooks, and gnats in bright array,
  And lordly beetles out for holiday;
And spiders small that work in silver sheen
To make a kirtle for the Fairy Queen,
  That she may don it on the First of May.

XIII.

I hear, in thought, I hear the very words
  That Arethusa, turn'd into a brook,
  Spoke to Diana, when her leave she took
Of all she lov'd—low-weeping as the birds
Shrill'd out of tune, and all the frighten'd herds
  Scamper'd to death, in spite of pipe and crook.

XIV.

I know, to-day, why winds were made to sigh
  And why they hide themselves, and why they gloat
  In some old ruin! Mote confers with mote,
And shell with shell; and corals live and die,
And die and live, below the deep. And why?
  To make a necklace for my lady's throat.

xv.

And yet the world, in all its varied girth,
  Lacks what we look for.   There is something base
  In mere existence—something in the face
Of men and women which accepts the earth,
And all its havings, as its right of birth,
  But not its quittance, not its resting-place.

xvi.

There have been moments, at the set of sun,
  When I have long'd for wings upon the wind,
  That I might seek a planet to my mind,
More full-develop'd than this present one;
With more of scope, when all is said and done,
  To satisfy the wants of human kind.

xvii.

A world with thee, a home in some remote
  And unknown region, which no sage's ken
  Has compass'd yet; of which no human pen
Has traced the limits; where no terrors float
In wind or wave, and where the soul may note
  A thousand raptures unreveal'd to men.

XVIII.

To be transported in a magic car,
  On some transcendent night in early June,
  Beyond the horn'd projections of the moon;
To have our being in a bridal star,
In lands of light, where only angels are,
  Athwart the spaces where the comets swoon.

XIX.

To be all this: to have in our estate
  Worlds without stint, and quit them for the clay
  Of some new planet where a summer's day
Lasts fifty years; and there to celebrate
Our Golden Wedding, by the will of Fate—
  This were a subject for a seraph's lay.

XX.

This were a life to live,—a life indeed,—
  A thing to die for; if, in truth, we die
  When we but put our mortal vestments by.
This were a climax for a lover's need
Sweeter than songs, and holier than the creed
  Of half the zealots who have sought the sky.

Letter
VIII
A VISION

LETTER VIII.

A VISION.

I.

YES, I will tell thee what, a week ago,
  I dreamt of thee, and all the joy therein
  Which I conceiv'd, and all the holy din
Of throbbing music, which appear'd to flow
From room to room, as if to make me know
  The power thereof to lead me out of sin.

II.

Methought I saw thee in a ray of light,
  This side a grove—a dream within a dream—
  With eyes of tender pleading, and the gleam
Of far-off summers in thy tresses bright ;
And I did tremble at the gracious sight,
  As one who sees a naïad in a stream.

III.

I follow'd thee.   I knew that, in the wood,
   Where thus we met, there was a trysting-place.
   I follow'd thee, as mortals in a chase
Follow the deer.   I knew that it was good
To track thy step, and promptly understood
   The fitful blush that flutter'd to thy face.

IV.

I followed thee to where a brook did run
   Close to a grot; and there I knelt to thee.
   And then a score of birds flew over me,—
Birds which arrived because the day was done,
To sing the Sanctus of the setting sun;
   And then I heard thy voice upon the lea.

V.

" Follow! " it cried.   I rose and follow'd fast;
   And, in my dream, I felt the dream was true,
   And that, full soon, Titania, with her crew
Of imps and fays, would meet me on the blast.
But this was hindered; and I quickly passed
   Into the valley where the cedars grew.

VI.

And what a scene, O God! and what repose,
  And what sad splendour in the burning west:
  A languid sun low-dropping to his rest,
And incense rising, as of old it rose,
To do him honour at the daylight's close,—
  The birds entranced, and all the winds repress'd.

VII.

I followed thee.   I came to where a shrine
  Stood in the trees, and where an oaken gate
  Swung in the air, so turbulent of late.
I touch'd thy hand; it quiver'd into mine;
And then I look'd into thy face benign,
  And saw the smile for which the angels wait.

VIII.

And lo! the moon had sailed into the main
  Of that blue sky, as if therein did poise
  A silver boat; and then a tuneful noise
Broke from the copse where late a breeze was slain;
And nightingales, in ecstasy of pain,
  Did break their hearts with singing the old joys.

IX.

" Is this the spot ? " I cried, " is this the spot
    Where I must tell thee all my heart's desire?
    Is this the time when I must drink the fire,
And eat the snow, and find it fever-hot?
I freeze with heat, and yet I fear it not;
    And all my pulses thrill me like a lyre."

X.

A wondrous light was thrown upon thy face;
    It was the light within; it was the ray
    Of thine own soul. And then a voice did say,
" Glory to God the King, and Jesu's grace
Here and hereafter!" and about the place
    A radiance shone surpassing that of day.

XI.

It was thy voice.   It was the voice I prize
    More than the sound of April in the dales,
    More than the songs of larks and nightingales,
And more than the teachings of the worldly-wise.
" Glory to God," it said, " for in the skies,
    And here on earth, 'tis He alone prevails."

A VISION.

XII.

And then I asked thee: " Shall I tell thee now
  All that I think of, when, by land and sea,
  The days and nights illume the world for me ?
And how I muse on marriage, as I bow
In God's own places, with a throbbing brow ?
    And how, at night, I dream of kissing thee ? "

XIII.

But thou did'st answer: " First behold this man !
  He is thy lord, for love's and lady's sake;
  He is thy master, or I much mistake."
And I perceiv'd, hard by, a phantom wan
And wild and kingly, who did, walking, span
  The open space that lay beside the brake.

XIV.

It was Beethoven.   It was he who came
  From monstrous shades, to journey yet awhile
  In pleasant nooks, and vainly seek the smile
Of one lov'd woman—she to whom his fame
Had been a glory had she sought the same,
  And lov'd a soul so grand, so free from guile.

XV.

It was the Kaiser of the land of song,
  The giant-singer who did storm the gates
  Of Heaven and Hell, a man to whom the Fates
Were fierce as furies, and who suffer'd wrong
And ached and bore it, and was brave and strong,
  But gaunt as ocean when its rage abates.

XVI.

I knew his tread.   I knew him by his look
  Of pent-up sorrow—by his hair unkempt
  And torn attire—and by his smile exempt
From all but pleading.   Yet his body shook
With some great joy; and onward he betook
  His echoing steps the way that I had dreamt.

XVII.

I bow'd my head.   The lordly being pass'd.
  He was my king, and I did bow to him.
  And when I rais'd mine eyes they were as dim
As tears could make them.   And the moon, aghast,
Glared in the sky ; and westward came a blast
  Which shook the earth like shouts of cherubim.

XVIII.

I held my breath.   I could have fled the place,
  As men have fled before the wrath of God.
  But I beheld my Lady where she trod
The darken'd path; and I did cry apace:
"Help me, my Lady!" and thy lustrous face
  Gladden'd the air, and quicken'd all the sod.

XIX.

Then did I hear again that voice of cheer.
  "Lovest thou me," it said, "or music best?"
  I seized thy hand, I drew thee to my breast.
"Thee, only thee!" I cried.   "From year to year,
Thee, only thee—not fame!" And silver-clear,
  Thy voice responded: "God will grant the rest."

XX.

I kiss'd thine eyes.   I kiss'd them where the blue
  Peep'd smiling forth; and proudly as before
  I heard the tones that thrill'd me to the core.
"If thou love me," they said, "if thou be true,
Thou shalt have fame, and love, and music too!"
  Entranced I kiss'd the lips that I adore.

LETTER IX.

TO-MORROW.

I.

O LOVE! O Love! O Gateway of Delight!
Thou porch of peace, thou pageant of the prime
Of all God's creatures! I am here to climb
Thine upward steps, and daily and by night
To gaze beyond them, and to search aright
The far-off splendour of thy track sublime.

II.

For, in thy precincts, on the further side,
Beyond the turret where the bells are rung,
Beyond the chapel where the rites are sung,
There is a garden fit for any bride.
O Love! by thee, by thee are sanctified
The joys thereof to keep our spirits young.

83

III.

By thee, dear Love! by thee, if all be well—
   And we be wise enough to own the touch
   Of some bright folly that has thrill'd us much—
By thee, till death, we may regain the spell
Of wizard Merlin, and in every dell
   Confront a Muse, and bow to it as such.

IV.

Love! Happy Love! Behold me where I stand
   This side thy portal, with my straining eyes
   Turn'd to the Future. Cloudless are the skies,
And, far adown the road which thou hast spann'd,
I see the groves of that elected land
   Which is the place I call my paradise.

V.

But what is this? The plains are known to me;
   The hills are known, the fields, the little fence,
   The noisy brook as clear as innocence,
And this old oak, the wonder of the lea,
Which stops the wind to know if there shall be
   Sorrow for men, or pride, or recompense.

VI.

I know these things, yet hold it little blame
  To know them not, though in their proud array,
  The flowers advance to make the world so gay.
Ah, what a change! The things I know by name
Look unfamiliar all, and, like a flame,
  The roses burn upon the hedge to-day.

VII.

The grass is velvet. There are pearls thereon,
  And golden signs, and braid that doth appear
  Made for a bridal. This is fairy gear
If I mistake not. I shall know anon.
Nature herself will teach me how to con
  The new-found words to thank the glowing year.

VIII.

This is the path that led me to the brook;
  And this the mead, and this the mossy slope,
  And this the place where breezes did elope
With giddy moths, enamour'd of a look;
And here I sat alone, or with a book,
  Dreaming the dreams of constancy and hope.

IX.

I loved the river well; but not till now
  Did I perceive the marvels of the shore.
  This is a cave, and this an emerald floor;
And here Sir Englantine might make a vow,
And here a king, a guilty king, might bow
  Before a child, and break his word no more.

X.

The day is dying. I shall see him die,
  And I shall watch the sunset, and the red
  Of all that splendour when the day is dead.
And I shall see the stars upon the sky,
And think them torches that are lit on high
  To light the Lord Apollo to his bed.

XI.

And sweet To-morrow, like a golden bark,
  Will call for me, and lead me on apace
  To where I shall behold, in all her grace,
Mine own true Lady, whom a happy lark
Did late salute, appointing, after dark,
  A nightingale to carol in his place.

XII.

Oh, come to me! Oh, come, belovèd day,
  O sweet To-morrow! Youngest of the sons
  Of old King Time, to whom Creation runs
As men to God. Oh, quickly with thy ray
Anoint my head, and teach me how to pray,
  As gentle Jesus taught the little ones.

XIII.

I am aweary of the waiting hours,
  I am aweary of the tardy night.
  The hungry moments rob me of delight,
The crawling minutes steal away my powers;
And I am sick at heart, as one who cowers,
  In lonely haunts, remov'd from human sight.

XIV.

How shall I think the night was meant for sleep,
  When I must count the dreadful hours thereof,
  And cannot beat them down, or bid them doff
Their hateful masks? A man may wake and weep
From hour to hour, and, in the silence deep,
  See shadows move, and almost hear them scoff.

XV.

Oh, come to me, To-morrow! like a friend,
  And not as one who bideth for the clock.
  Be swift to come, and I will hear thee knock,
And though the night refuse to make an end
Of her dull peace, I promptly will descend
  And let thee in, and thank thee for the shock.

XVI.

Dear, good To-morrow! in my life, till now,
  I did not think to need thee quite so soon.
  I did not think that I should hate the moon,
Or new or old, or that my fevered brow
Requir'd the sun to cool it.   I will bow
  To this new day, that he may grant the boon.

XVII.

Yes, 'twill consent.   The day will dawn at last.
  Day and the tide approach.   They cannot rest.
  They must approach.   They must by every test
Of all men's knowledge, neither slow nor fast,
Approach and front us.   When the night is past,
  The morrow's dawn will lead me to my quest.

XVIII.

Then shall I tremble greatly, and be glad,
  For I shall meet my true-love all alone,
  And none shall tell me of her dainty zone,
And none shall say how sweetly she is clad;
But I shall know it. Men may call me mad;
  But I shall know how bright the world has grown.

XIX.

There is a grammar of the lips and eyes,
  And I have learnt it. There are tokens sure
  Of trust in love; and I have found them pure.
Is love the guerdon then ? Is love the prize ?
It is! It is! We find it in the skies,
  And here on earth 'tis all that will endure.

XX.

All things for love. All things in some divine
  And wish'd for way, conspire, as Nature knows,
  To some great good. Where'er a daisy grows
There grows a joy. The forest-trees combine
To talk of peace when mortals would repine;
  And he is false to God who flouts the rose.

Letter

X

A Retrospect

LETTER X.

———

I.

I WALK again beside the roaring sea,
  And once again I harken to the speech
  Of waves exulting on the madden'd beach.
A sound of awful joy it seems to me,
A shuddering sound of God's eternity,—
  Telling of things beyond the sage's reach.

II.

I walk alone.   I see the bounding waves
  Curl'd into foam.   I watch them as they leap
  Like wild sea-horses loosen'd from the deep.
And well I know that they have seen the graves
Of shipwreck'd sailors; for Disaster paves
  The fearful fields where reapers cannot reap.

III.

Out there, in islands where the summer sun
  Goes down in tempest, there are loathsome things
  That crawl to shore, and flap unsightly wings.
But here there are no monsters that can run
To catch the limbs of bathers; no! not one;
  And here the wind is harmless when it stings.

IV.

There is a glamour all about the bay,
  As if the nymphs of Greece had tarried here.
  The sands are golden, and the rocks appear
Crested with silver; and the breezes play
Snatches of song they humm'd when far away,
  And then are hush'd, as if from sudden fear.

V.

They think of thee.   They hunt; they meditate.
  They will not quit the shore till they have seen
  The very spot where thou did'st stand serene
In all thy beauty; and of me they prate,
Knowing I love thee.   And, like one elate,
  The grand old sea remembers what hath been.

VI.

How many hours, how many days we met
 Here on the beach, in that delirious time
 When all the waves appear'd to break in rhyme.
Life was a joy, and love was like a debt
Paid and repaid in kisses—good to get,
 And good to lose—unhoarded, yet sublime.

VII.

We wander'd here. We saw the tide advance,
 We saw it ebb. We saw the widow'd shore
 Waiting for Ocean with its organ roar,
Knowing that, day by day, through happy chance,
She would be wooed anew, amid the dance
 Of bridal waves high-bounding as before.

VIII.

And I remember how, at flush of morn,
 Thou didst depart alone, to find a nook
 Where none could see thee; where a lover's look
Were profanation worse than any scorn;
And how I went my way, among the corn,
 To wait for thee beside the Shepherd's brook.

IX.

And lo! from out a cave thou didst emerge,
  Sweet as thyself, the flower of Womankind.
  I know 'twas thus; for, in my secret mind,
I see thee now.   I see thee in the surge
Of those wild waves, well knowing that they urge
  Some idle wish, untalk'd-of to the wind.

X.

I think the beach was thankful to have known
  Thy warm, white body, and the blessedness
  Of thy first shiver; and I well can guess
How, when thy limbs were toss'd and overthrown,
The sea was pleased, and every smallest stone,
  And every wave, was proud of thy caress.

XI.

A maiden diving, with dishevell'd hair,
  Sheer from a rock; a syren of the deep
  Call'd into action, ere a wave could leap
Breast-high to daunt her; Daphne, by a prayer,
Lured from a forest for the sea to bear—
  This were a dream to fill a poet's sleep.

XII.

This were a thing for Phœbus to have eyed;
    And he did eye it.   Yea, the Deathless One
    Did eye thy beauty.   It was madly done.
He saw thee in the rising of the tide.
He saw thee well.   The truth is not denied:
    The shore was proud to show thee to the sun.

XIII.

Never since Venus, at a god's decree,
    Uprose from ocean, has there lived on earth
    A face like thine, a form of so much worth;
And nowhere has the moon-obeying sea
Known such perfection, down from head to knee,
    And knee to foot, since that Olympian birth.

XIV.

And, sooth, the moon was anxious to have placed
    Her head beside thee, on the waters bright.
    But she was foil'd; for thou so late at night
Wouldst not go forth: no! not to be embraced
By Nature's Queen, though, round about the waist,
    She would have ring'd thee with her softest light.

XV.

Ah me! had I a lute of sovereign power
    I would enlarge on this, and plainly show
    That there is nothing like thee here below,—
Nothing so comely, nothing in its dower
Of youth and grace, so like a human flower,
    And white withal, and guiltless as the snow.

XVI.

For thou art fair as lilies, with the flush
    That roses have while waiting for a kiss;
    And when thou smilest nothing comes amiss.
The earth is glad to see thy dimpled blush.
Had I the lute of Orpheus I would hush
    All meaner sounds to tell the stars of this.

XVII.

I would, I swear, by Pallas' own consent,
    Inform all creatures whom the stars behold
    That thou art mine, and that a pen of gold,
With ink of fire, though by an angel lent,
Were all too poor to tell my true content,
    And how I love thee seven times seventy fold.

XVIII.

And sure am I that, in the ancient days,
    Achilles heard no voice so passing sweet,
    And none so trancing, none that could compete
With thine for fervour; none, in watery ways
Where Neptune dwelt, so worthy of the praise
    Of Thetis' son, the sure and swift of feet.

XIX.

He never met upon the plains of Troy
    Goddess or maiden so divinely fraught.
    Not Helen's self, for whom the Trojans fought,
Was like to thee.   Her love had much alloy,
But thine has none.   Her beauty was a toy,
    But thine's a gem, unsullied and unbought.

XX.

And ne'er was seen by poet, in a sweven,
    An eye like thine, a face so fair to see
    As that which makes the sunlight sweet to me.
Nor need I wait for death, or for the levin
In yonder cloud, to find the path to Heaven.
    It fronts me here.   'Tis manifest in thee!

Letter

XI

FAITH

LETTER XI.

———

I.

NOW will I sing to God a song of praise,
  And thank the morning for the light it brings,
    Aye! and the earth for every flower that springs,
And every tree that, in the jocund days,
Thrills to the blast. My voice I will upraise
  To thank the world for every bird that sings.

II.

I will unpack my mind of all its fears,
  I will advance to where the matin fires
    Absorb the hills. My hopes and my desires
Will lead me safe; and day will have no tears
And night no torture, as in former years,
  To warp my nature when my soul aspires.

III.

I will endure.   I will not strive to peep
   Behind the barriers of the days to come,
   Nor, adding up the figures of a sum,
Dispose of prayers as men dispose of sleep.
I cannot count the stars, or walk the deep;
   But I can pray, and Faith shall not be dumb.

IV.

I take myself and thee as mine estate—
   Thee and myself.   The world is centred there.
   If thou be well I know the skies are fair;
If not, they press me down with leaden weight,
And all is dark; and morning comes too late;
   And all the birds are tuneless in the air.

V.

I need but thee: thee only.   Thou alone
   Art all my joy: a something to the sight
   As grand as Silence, and as snowy white.
And do thou pardon if I make it known,
As oft I do, with mine Amati's tone,
   Amid the stillness of the starry night.

VI.

Oh, give me pity of thy heart and mind,
　　Mine own sweet Lady, if I vex thee now.
　　If the repeating of my constant vow
Be undesired, have pity! I were blind,
And deaf and dumb, and mad, were I inclined
　　To curb my feelings when to thee I bow.

VII.

Forgive the challenge of my longing lips
　　If these offend thee; and forgive me, too,
　　If I perceive, within thine eyes of blue,
More than I utter—more than, in eclipse,
A man may note atween the argent tips
　　Of frighted Dian whom the Fates pursue.

VIII.

It is the thing I dream of; 'tis the thing
　　We know as rapture, when, with sudden thrill,
　　It snares the heart and subjugates the will;
I mean the pride, the power, by which we cling
To natures nobler than the ones we bring,
　　To keep entire the fire we cannot chill.

IX.

Coyest of nymphs, my Lady! whom I seek
As sailors seek salvation out at sea,
And poets fame, and soldiers victory,
Behold! I note the blush upon thy cheek,
The flag of truce that tells me thou art meek
And soon wilt yield thy fortress up to me.

X.

It is thy soul; it is thy soul in arms
Which thus I conquer. All thy furtive sighs,
And all the glances of thy wistful eyes,
Proclaim the swift surrender of thy charms.
I kiss thy hand; and tremors and alarms
Discard, in parting, all their late disguise.

XI.

They were not foes. They knew me, one and all;
They knew I lov'd thee, and they lured me on
To try my fortune, and to wait thereon
For just reward. The scaling of the wall
Was not the meed; there came the festival,
And now there comes the crown that I must don.

XII.

O my Belovèd! I am king of thee,
  And thou my queen; and I will wear the crown
  A little moment, for thy love's renown.
Yea, for a moment, it shall circle me,
And then be thine, so thou, upon thy knee,
  Do seek the same, with all thy tresses down.

XIII.

For woman still is mistress of the man,
  Though man be master. 'Tis the woman's right
  To choose her king, and crown him in her sight,
And make him feel the pressure of the span
Of her soft arms, as only woman can;
  For, with her weakness, she excels his might.

XIV.

It is her joy indeed to be so frail
  That he must shield her; he of all the world
  Whom most she loves; and then, if he be hurl'd
To depths of sorrow, she will more avail
Than half a senate. Troubles may assail,
  But she will guide him by her lips impearl'd.

XV.

A woman clung to Cæsar; he was great,
  And great the power he gain'd by sea and land.
  But when he wrong'd her, when he spurn'd the hand
Which once he knelt to, when he scoff'd at Fate,
Glory dispers'd, and left him desolate;
  For God remember'd all that first was plann'd.

XVI.

The cannon's roar, the wisdom of the sage,
  The strength of armies, and the thrall of kings—
  All these are weak compared to weaker things.
Napoleon fell because, in puny rage,
He wrong'd his house; and earth became a cage
  For this poor eagle with his batter'd wings.

XVII.

Believe me, Love! I honour, night and day,
  The name of Woman. 'Tis the nobler sex.
  Villains may shame it; sorrows may perplex;
But still 'tis watchful. Man may take away
All its possessions, all its worldly sway,
  And yet be worshipp'd by the soul he wrecks.

XVIII.

A word of love to Woman is as sweet
  As nectar'd rapture in a golden bowl;
  And when she quaffs the heavens asunder roll,
And God looks through. And, from his judgment-seat,
He blesses those who part, and those who meet,
  And those who join the links of soul with soul.

XIX.

And are there none untrue ? God knows there are!
  Aye, there are those who learn in time the laugh
  That ends in madness—women who for chaff
Have sold their corn—who seek no guiding-star,
And find no faith to light them from afar;
  Of whom 'tis said: " They need no epitaph."

XX.

All this is known; but lo! for sake of One
  Who lives in glory—for my mother's sake,
  For thine, and hers, O Love!—I pity take
On all poor women. Jesu's will be done!
Honour for all, and infamy for none,
  This side the borders of the burning lake.

Letter
XII
VICTORY

LETTER XII.

VICTORY.

I.

NOW have I reach'd the goal of my desire,
  For thou hast sworn—as sweetly as a bell
  Makes out its chime—the oath I love to tell,
The fealty-oath of which I never tire.
The lordly forest seems a giant's lyre,
  And sings, and rings, the thoughts that o'er it swell.

II.

The air is fill'd with voices.   I have found
  Comfort at last, enthralment, and a joy
  Past all belief; a peace without alloy.
There is a splendour all about the ground
As if from Eden, when the world was drown'd,
  Something had come which death could not destroy.

III.

It seems, indeed, as if to me were sent
    A smile from Heaven—as if to-day the clods
    Were lined with silk—the trees divining rods,
And roses gems for some high tournament.
I should not be so proud, or so content,
    If I could sup, to-night, with all the gods.

IV.

A shrinèd saint would change his place with me
    If he but knew the worth of what I feel.
    He is enrobed indeed, and for his weal
Hath much concern; but how forlorn is he!
How pale his pomp! He cannot sue to thee,
    But I am sainted every time I kneel.

V.

I walk'd abroad, to-day, ere yet the dark
    Had left the hills, and down the beaten road
    I saunter'd forth a mile from mine abode.
I heard, afar, the watchdog's sudden bark,
And, near at hand, the tuning of a lark,
    Safe in its nest, but weighted with an ode.

VI.

The moon was pacing up the sky serene,
   Pallid and pure, as if she late had shown
   Her outmost side, and fear'd to make it known;
And, like a nun, she gazed upon the scene
From bars of cloud that seemed to stand between,
   And pray'd and smiled, and smiled and pray'd alone.

VII.

The stars had fled. Not one remain'd behind
   To warn or comfort; or to make amends
   For hope delay'd,—for ecstasy that ends
At dawn's approach. The firmament was blind
Of all its eyes; and, wanton up the wind,
   There came the shuddering that the twilight sends.

VIII.

The hills exulted at the Morning's birth,—
   And clouds assembled, quick, as heralds run
   Before a king to say the fight is won.
The rich, warm daylight fell upon the earth
Like wine outpour'd in madness, or in mirth,
   To celebrate the rising of the sun.

IX.

And when the soaring lark had done its prayer,
   The holy thing, self-poised amid the blue
   Of that great sky, did seem, a space or two,
To pause and think, and then did clip the air
And dropped to earth to claim his guerdon there.
   "Thank God!" I cried, "My dearest dream is true!"

X.

I was too happy, then, to leap and dance;
   But I could ponder; I could gaze and gaze
   From earth to sky and back to woodland ways.
The bird had thrill'd my heart, and cheer'd my glance,
For he had found to-day his nest-romance,
   And lov'd a mate, and crown'd her with his praise.

XI.

O Love! my Love! I would not for a throne,
   I would not for the thrones of all the kings
   Who yet have liv'd, or for a seraph's wings,
Or for the nod of Jove when night hath flown,
Consent to rule an empire all alone.
   No! I must have the grace of our two rings.

XII.

I must possess thee from the crowning curl
  Down to the feet, and from the beaming eye
  Down to the bosom where my treasures lie.
From blush to blush, and from the rows of pearl
That light thy smile, I must possess thee, girl,
  And be thy lord and master till I die.

XIII.

This, and no less: the keeper of thy fame,
  The proud controller of each silken tress,
  And each dear item of thy loveliness,
And every oath, and every dainty name
Known to a bride: a picture in a frame
  Of golden hair, to turn to and caress.

XIV.

And though I know thee prone, in vacant hours,
  To laugh and talk with those who circumvent
  And make mad speeches; though I know the bent
Of some such men, and though in ladies' bowers
They brag of swords—I know my proven powers;
  I know myself and thee, and am content.

XV.

I know myself; and why should I demur?
  The lily, bowing to the breeze's play,
  Is not forgetful of the sun in May.
She is his nymph, and with a servitor
She doth but jest. The sun looks down at her,
  And knows her true, and loves her day by day.

XVI.

E'en so I thee, O Lady of my Heart!
  O Lady white as lilies on the lea,
  And fair as foam upon the ocean free
Whereon the sun hath sent a shining dart!
E'en so I love thee, blameless as thou art,
  And with my soul's desire I compass thee.

XVII.

For thou art Woman in the sweetest sense
  Of true endowment, and a bride indeed
  Fit for Apollo. This is Woman's need:
To be a beacon when the air is dense,
A bower of peace, a life-long recompense —
  This is the sum of Woman's worldly creed.

XVIII.

And what is Man the while ?   And what his will ?
  And what the furtherance of his earthly hope ?
  To turn to Faith, to turn, as to a rope
A drowning sailor; all his blood to spill
For One he loves, to keep her out of ill—
  This is the will of Man, and this his scope.

XIX.

'Tis like the tranquil sea, that knows anon
  It can be wild, and keep away from home
  A thousand ships—and lash itself to foam—
And beat the shore, and all that lies thereon—
And catch the thunder ere the flash has gone
  Forth from the cloud that spans it like a dome.

XX.

This is the will of Man, and this is mine.
  But lo! I love thee more than wealth or fame,
  More than myself, and more than those who came
With Christ's commission from the goal divine.
Soul of my soul, and mine as I am thine,
  I cling to thee, my Life! as fire to flame.

Miscellaneous Poems.

ANTEROS.

THIS is the feast-day of my soul and me,
   For I am half a god and half a man.
These are the hours in which are heard by sea,
By land and wave, and in the realms of space,
   The lute-like sounds which sanctify my span,
And give me power to sway the human race.

II.

I am the king whom men call Lucifer,
   I am the genius of the nether spheres.
Give me my Christian name, and I demur.
Call me a Greek, and straightway I rejoice.
   Yea, I am Anteros, and with my tears
I salt the earth that gladdens at my voice.

ANTEROS.

III.

I am old Anteros; a young, old god;
   A sage who smiles and limps upon a crutch.
But I can turn my crutch into a rod,
And change my rod into a crown of wood.
   Yea, I am he who conquers with a touch,
And plays with poisons till he makes them good.

IV.

The sun, uprising with his golden hair,
   Is mine apostle; and he serves me well.
Thoughts and desires of mine, beyond compare,
Thrill at his touch. The moon, so lost in thought,
   Has pined for love; and wanderers out of hell,
And saints from heaven, have known what I have
      taught.

V.

Great are my griefs; my joys are multiplex;
   And beasts and birds and men my subjects are;
Yea, all created things that have a sex,
And flies and flowers and monsters of the mere;
   All these, and more, proclaim me from afar,
And sing my marriage songs from year to year.

VI.

There are no bridals but the ones I make;
   For men are quicken'd when they turn to me.
The soul obeys me for its body's sake,
And each is form'd for each, as day for night.
   'Tis but the soul can pay the body's fee
To win the wisdom of a fool's delight.

VII.

Yea, this is so. My clerks have set it down,
   And birds have blabbed it to the winds of heaven.
The flowers have guessed it, and, in bower and town,
Lovers have sung the songs that I have made.
   Give me your lives, O mortals, and, for leaven,
Ye shall receive the fires that cannot fade.

VIII.

O men! O maidens! O ye listless ones!
   Ye who desert my temples in the East,
Ye who reject the rays of summer suns,
And cling to shadows in the wilderness;
   Why are ye sad? Why frown ye at the feast,
Ye who have eyes to see and lips to press?

IX.

Why, for a wisdom that ye will not prove,
   A joy that crushes and a love that stings,
A freak, a frenzy in a fated groove,
A thing of nothing born of less than nought—
   Why in your hearts do ye desire these things,
Ye who abhor the joys that ye have sought?

X.

See, see! I weep, but I can jest at times;
   Yea, I can dance and toss my tears away.
The sighs I breathe are fragrant as the rhymes
Of men and maids whose hearts are overthrown.
   I am the God for whom all maidens pray,
But none shall have me for herself alone.

XI.

No; I have love enough, here where I stand,
   To marry fifty maids in their degree;
Aye, fifty times five thousand in a band,
And every bride the proxy of a score.
   Want ye a mate for millions ?   I am he.
Glory is mine, and glee-time evermore.

XII.

O men! O masters!   O ye kings of grief!
  Ye who control the world but not the grave,
What have ye done to make delight so brief,
Ye who have spurn'd the minstrel and the lyre?
  I will not say: "Be patient."   Ye are brave;
And ye shall guess the pangs of my desire.

XIII.

There shall be traitors in the court of love,
  And tears and torture and the bliss of pain.
The maids of men shall seek the gods above,
And drink the nectar of the golden lake.
  Blessed are they for whom the gods are fain;
They shall be glad for love's and pity's sake.

XIV.

They shall be taught the songs the syrens know,
  The wave's lament, the west wind's psalmistry,
The secrets of the south and of the snow,
The wherewithal of day, and death, and night.
  O men! O maidens! pray no prayer for me,
But sing to me the songs of my delight.

XV.

Aye, sing to me the songs I love to hear,
    And let the sound thereof ascend to heaven.
And let the singers, with a voice of cheer,
Announce my name to all the ends of earth;
    And let my servants, seventy times and seven,
Re-shout the raptures of my Samian mirth!

XVI.

Let joy prevail, and Frenzy, like a flame,
    Seize all the souls of men for sake of me.
For I will have Contention put to shame,
And all the hearts of all things comforted.
    There are no laws but mine on land and sea,
And men shall crown me when their kings are dead.

THE WAKING OF THE LARK.

I.

O BONNIE bird, that in the brake, exultant, dost
   prepare thee—
As poets do whose thoughts are true, for wings that will
   upbear thee—
      Oh ! tell me, tell me, bonnie bird,
      Canst thou not pipe of hope deferred?
Or canst thou sing of naught but Spring among the golden
   meadows ?

II.

Methinks a bard (and thou art one) should suit his song
   to sorrow,
And tell of pain, as well as gain, that waits us on the
   morrow;
      But thou art not a prophet, thou,
      If naught but joy can touch thee now;
If, in thy heart, thou hast no vow that speaks of Nature's
   anguish.

III.

Oh ! I have held my sorrows dear, and felt, tho' poor and
    slighted,
The songs we love are those we hear when love is unre-
    quited.
        But thou art still the slave of dawn,
        And canst not sing till night be gone,
Till o'er the pathway of the fawn the sunbeams shine and
    quiver.

IV.

Thou art the minion of the sun that rises in his splendour,
And canst not spare for Dian fair the songs that should
    attend her.
        The moon, so sad and silver-pale,
        Is mistress of the nightingale;
And thou wilt sing on hill and dale no ditties in the
    darkness.

V.

For Queen and King thou wilt not spare one note of thine
    outpouring;
Thou art as free as breezes be on Nature's velvet flooring.
        The daisy, with its hood undone,
        The grass, the sunlight, and the sun—
These are the joys, thou holy one, that pay thee for thy
    singing.

VI.

Oh, hush! Oh, hush! how wild a gush of rapture in the
distance,—
A roll of rhymes, a toll of chimes, a cry for love's assist-
ance;
> A sound that wells from happy throats,
> A flood of song where beauty floats,
And where our thoughts, like golden boats, do seem to
cross a river.

VII.

This is the advent of the lark—the priest in gray apparel—
Who doth prepare to trill in air his sinless Summer carol;
> This is the prelude to the lay
> The birds did sing in Cæsar's day,
And will again, for aye and aye, in praise of God's
creation.

VIII.

O dainty thing, on wonder's wing, by life and love elated,
Oh! sing aloud from cloud to cloud, till day be conse-
crated;
> Till from the gateways of the morn,
> The sun, with all his light unshorn,
His robes of darkness round him torn, doth scale the lofty
heavens!

A BALLAD OF KISSES.

-- -- -- --

I.

THERE are three kisses that I call to mind,
    And I will sing their secrets as I go.
The first, a kiss too courteous to be kind,
    Was such a kiss as monks and maidens know;
    As sharp as frost, as blameless as the snow.

II.

The second kiss, ah God! I feel it yet,
    And evermore my soul will loathe the same.
The toys and joys of fate I may forget,
    But not the touch of that divided shame:
    It clove my lips; it burnt me like a flame.

III.

The third, the final kiss, is one I use
    Morning and noon and night; and not amiss.
Sorrow be mine if such I do refuse!
    And when I die, be love, enrapt in bliss,
    Re-sanctified in Heaven by such a kiss.

MARY ARDEN.

I.

O THOU to whom, athwart the perish'd days
    And parted nights long sped, we lift our gaze,
Behold! I greet thee with a modern rhyme,
Love-lit and reverent as befits the time,
    To solemnize the feast-day of thy son.

II.

And who was he who flourish'd in the smiles
Of thy fair face? 'Twas Shakespeare of the Isles,
Shakespeare of England, whom the world has known
As thine, and ours, and Glory's, in the zone
    Of all the seas and all the lands of earth.

III.

He was un-famous when he came to thee,
But sound, and sweet, and good for eyes to see,
And born at Stratford, on St. George's Day,
A week before the wondrous month of May;
   And God therein was gracious to us all.

IV.

He lov'd thee, Lady! and he lov'd the world;
And, like a flag, his fealty was unfurl'd;
And Kings who flourished ere thy son was born
Shall live through him, from morn to furthest morn,
   In all the far-off cycles yet to come.

V.

He gave us Falstaff, and a hundred quips,
A hundred mottoes from immortal lips;
And, year by year, we smile to keep away
The generous tears that mind us of the sway
   Of his great singing, and the pomp thereof.

VI.

His was the nectar of the gods of Greece,
The lute of Orpheus, and the Golden Fleece
Of grand endeavour; and the thunder-roll
Of words majestic, which, from pole to pole,
　Have borne the tidings of our English tongue.

VII.

He gave us Hamlet; and he taught us more
Than schools have taught us; and his fairy-lore
Was fraught with science; and he called from death
Verona's Lovers, with the burning breath
　Of their great passion that has filled the spheres.

VIII.

He made us know Cordelia, and the man
Who murder'd sleep, and baleful Caliban;
And, one by one, athwart the gloom appear'd
Maidens and men and myths who were revered
　In olden days, before the earth was sad.

IX.

Aye! this is true.   It was ordainèd so;
He was thine own, three hundred years ago;
But ours to-day; and ours till earth be red
With doom-day splendour for the quick and dead,
  And days and nights are scattered like the leaves.

X.

It was for this he lived, for this he died;
To raise to Heaven the face that never lied,
To lean to earth the lips that should become
Fraught with conviction when the mouth was dumb,
  And all the firm, fine body turn'd to clay.

XI.

He lived to seal, and sanctify the lives
Of perish'd maids, and uncreated wives,
And gave them each a space wherein to dwell;
And for his mother's sake he loved them well,
  And made them types, undying, of all truth.

XII.

O fair and fond young mother of the boy
Who wrought all this—O Mary!—in thy joy
Did'st thou perceive, when, fitful from his rest,
He turn'd to thee, that his would be the best
    Of all men's chanting since the world began?

XIII.

Did'st thou, O Mary! with the eye of trust
Perceive, prophetic, through the dark and dust
Of things terrene, the glory of thy son,
And all the pride therein that should be won
    By toilsome men, content to be his slaves?

XIV.

Did'st thou, good mother! in the tender ways
That women find to fill the fleeting days,
Behold afar the Giant who should rise
With foot on earth, and forehead in the skies,
    To write his name, and thine, among the stars?

XV.

I love to think it; and, in dreams at night
I see thee stand, erect, and all in white,
With hands out-yearning to that mighty form,
As if to draw him back from out the storm,—
    A child again, and thine to nurse withal.

XVI.

I see thee, pale and pure, with flowing hair,
And big, bright eyes, far-searching in the air
For thy sweet babe, and, in a trice of time,
I see the child advance to thee, and climb,
    And call thee " Mother!" in ecstatic tones.

XVII.

Yet, if my thought be vain—if, by a touch
Of this weak hand, I vex thee overmuch—
Forbear the blame, sweet Spirit! and endow
My heart with fervour while to thee I bow
    Athwart the threshold of my fading dream.

XVIII.

For, though so seeming-bold in this my song,
I turn to thee with reverence, in the throng
Of words and thoughts, as shepherds scann'd, afar,
The famed effulgence of that eastern star
　　Which usher'd in the Crown'd One of the heavens.

XIX.

In dreams of rapture I have seen thee pass
Along the banks of Avon, by the grass,
As fair as that fair Juliet whom thy son
Endow'd with life, but with the look of one
　　Who knows the nearest way to some new grave.

XX.

And often, too, I've seen thee in the flush
Of thy full beauty, while the mother's " Hush!"
Hung on thy lip, and all thy tangled hair
Re-clothed a bosom that in part was bare
　　Because a tiny hand had toy'd therewith!

XXI.

Oh! by the June-tide splendour of thy face
When, eight weeks old, the child in thine embrace
Did leap and laugh, O Mary! by the same,
I bow to thee, subservient to thy fame,
    And call thee England's Pride for evermore!

SACHAL.

A WAIF OF BATTLE.

I.

LO! at my feet,
     A something pale of hue;
A something sad to view;
Dead or alive I dare not call it sweet.

II.

Not white as snow;
Not transient as a tear!
A warrior left it here,
It was his passport ere he met the foe.

III.

Here is a name,
A word upon the book;
If ye but kneel to look,
Ye'll find the letters " Sachal " on the same.

IV.

His Land to cherish,
He died at twenty-seven.
There are no wars in Heaven,
But when he fought he gain'd the right to perish.

V.

Where was he born ?
In France, at Puy le Dôme.
A wanderer from his home,
He found a Fatherland beyond the morn.

VI.

'Twas France's plan;
The cause he did not ask.
His life was but a mask,
And he upraised it, martyr'd at Sedan.

VII.

And prone in death,
Beyond the name of France,
Beyond his hero-glance,—
He thought, belike, of her who gave him breath.

VIII.

O thou dead son!
O Sachal! far away,
But not forgot to-day,
I had a mother, too, but now have none.

IX.

Our hopes are brave.
Our faiths are braver still.
The soul shall no man kill;
For God will find us, each one in his grave.

X.

A land more vast
Than Europe's kingdoms are,—
A brighter, nobler star
Than victory's fearful light,—is thine at last.

XI.

And should'st thou meet
Yon Germans up on high,—
Thy foes when death was nigh,—
Nor thou nor they will sound the soul's retreat.

XII.

For all are just,
Yea, all are patriots there,
And thou, O Fils de Pierre!
Hast found thy marshal's baton in the dust.

XIII.

Oh, farewell, friend;
My friend, albeit unknown,
Save in thy death alone,
Oh, fare thee well till sin and sorrow end.

XIV.

In realms of joy
We'll meet; aye, every one:
Mother and sire and son,—
And my poor mother, too, will claim her boy.

XV.

Death leads to God.
Death is the Sword of Fate,
Death is the Golden Gate
That opens up to glory, through the sod.

XVI.

And thou that road,
O Sachal! thou hast found;
A king is not so crown'd
As thou art, soldier! in thy blest abode.

XVII.

Deathless in death,
Exalted, not destroy'd,
Thou art in Heaven employ'd
To swell the songs of angels with thy breath.

THE LADY OF THE MAY.

I.

O STARS that fade in amber skies
    Because ye dread the light of day,
O moon so lonely and so wise,
    Look down, and love my Love alwày;
    Salute the Lady of the May.

II.

O lark that soarest in the light
    To hail thy lord in his array,
Look down; be just; and sing aright.
    A lover claims thy song to-day
    To greet his Lady of the May.

III.

"O lady! lady!" sings the lark,
  " Thy lover's hest I do obey;
For thou art splendid after dark,
  And where thou smilest, there is day;
  And thou'rt the Lady of the May.

IV.

" The nightingale's a friend of mine,
  And yesternight she flew my way.
' Awake,' she cried, ' at morning shine
  And sing for me thy blythest lay
  To greet the Lady of the May.'

V.

" ' And tell her, tell her, gentle one,
  While thou attun'st thy morning lay,
That I will sing at set of sun
  Another song for thy sweet fay,
  Because she's Lady of the May.'

VI.

" And lo I come," the lark in air,
  Self-pois'd and free, did seem to say,
" I come to greet thy lady's hair
  And call its beams the light of day
  Which decks thy Lady of the May."

VII.

Oh, thank thee, bird that singest well!
  For all thou say'st and still would'st say
And for the thoughts which Philomel
  Intends to trill, in roundelay,
  To greet my Lady of the May.

VIII.

We two (my Love and I) are one,
  And so shall be, for aye and aye.
Go, take my homage to the sun,
  And bid him shine his best to-day,
  To crown my Lady of the May!

AN ODE TO ENGLISHMEN.

I WHO have sung of love and lady bright
  And mirth and music and the world's delight,
    Behold! to-day, I sound a sterner note
To move the minds of foemen when they fight.

Have I not said: There is no sweeter thing,
And none diviner than the wedding-ring?
    And, all intent to make my meaning plain,
Have I not kiss'd the lips of Love, the King?

Yea, this is so.   But lo! to-day there comes
The far-off sound of trumpets and of drums;
    And I must parley with the men of toil
Who rise in ranks exultant from the slums.

IV.

I must arraign each man; yea, all the host;
And each true soul shall learn the least and most
   Of all his wrongs,—if wrongs indeed they be;
And he shall face the flag that guards the coast.

V.

He shall salute it!   He shall find therein
Salve for his wounds and solace for his sin.
   Brother and guide is he who loves his Land;
But he is kinless who denies his kin.

VI.

Has he a heart to feel, a knee to bend,
And will not trust his country to the end?
   If this be so, God help him to a tear!
He shall be foiled, as foeman and as friend.

VII.

Bears he a sword?   I care not.   He is base;
Unfit to wield it, and of meaner place
   Than tongue can tell of, in the Senate House;
And he shall find no balm for his disgrace.

VIII.

O men! I charge ye, in the name of Him
Who rules the world, and guards the cherubim,
   I charge ye, pause, ere from the lighted track
Ye turn, distraught, to pathways that are dim.

IX.

Who gave your fathers, and your fathers' sons
The rights ye claim, amid the roar of guns,
   And 'mid the flash thereof from sea to sea?
Your country! through her lov'd, her chosen ones.

X.

Oh, ye are dastards if ye lift a hand,
Dastards and fools, if, loveless in a band,
   Ye touch in wrath the bulwark of the realm.
Ye shall be baulk'd, and Chivalry shall stand.

XI.

I have a sword, I also, and I swear
By my heart's faith, and by my Lady's hair,
   That I will strike the first of ye that moves,
If by a sign ye wrong the flag ye bear.

XII.

In Freedom's name, in her's to whom we bow,
In her great name, I charge ye, palter now
    With no traducer of your country's cause.
Accurst of God is he who breaks his vow!

ZULALIE.

I.

I AM the sprite
      That reigns at night,
My body is fair for man's delight.
      I leap and laugh
      As the wine I quaff,
And I am the queen of Astrofelle.

II.

      I curse and swear
      In my demon-lair;
I shake wild sunbeams out of my hair.
      I madden the old,
      I gladden the bold,
And I am the queen of Astrofelle.

III.

Of churchyard stone
I have made my throne;
My locks are looped with a dead man's bone.
Mine eyes are red
With the tears I shed,
And I am the queen of Astrofelle.

IV.

In cities and camps
I have lighted my lamps,
My kisses are caught by kings and tramps.
With rant and revel
My hair I dishevel,
And I am the queen of Astrofelle.

V.

My kisses are stains,
Mine arms are chains,
My forehead is fair and false like Cain's.
My gain is loss,
Mine honour is dross,—
And I am the queen of Astrofelle!

BEETHOVEN AT THE PIANO.

I.

SEE where Beethoven sits alone—a dream of days
  elysian,
A crownless king upon a throne, reflected in a vision—
The man who strikes the potent chords which make the
  world, in wonder,
Acknowledge him, though poor and dim, the mouthpiece
  of the thunder.

II.

He feels the music of the skies the while his heart is break-
  ing;
He sings the songs of Paradise, where love has no forsak-
  ing.
And, though so deaf he cannot hear the tempest as a
  token,
He makes the music of his mind the grandest ever
  spoken.

III.

He doth not hear the whispered word of love in his seclu-
  sion,
Or voice of friend, or song of bird, in Nature's sad confu-
  sion;
But he hath made, for Love's sweet sake, so wild a decla-
  mation
That all true lovers of the earth have claim'd him of their
  nation.

IV.

He had a Juliet in his youth, as Romeo had before him,
And, Romeo-like, he sought to die that she might then
  adore him;
But she was weak, as women are whose faith has not been
  proven,
And would not change her name for his—Guiciardi for
  Beethoven.

V.

O minstrel, whom a maiden spurned, but whom a world
  has treasured!
O sovereign of a greater realm than man has ever
  measured!
Thou hast not lost the lips of love, but thou hast gain'd, in
  glory,
The love of all who know the thrall of thine immortal
  story.

VI.

Thou art the bard whom none discard, but whom all men
  discover
To be a god, as Orpheus was, albeit a lonely lover;
A king to call the stones to life beside the roaring ocean,
And bid the stars discourse to trees in words of man's
  emotion.

VII.

A king of joys, a prince of tears, an emperor of the seasons,
Whose songs are like the sway of years in Love's immortal
  reasons;
A bard who knows no life but this: to love and be
  rejected,
And reproduce in earthly strains the prayers of the
  elected.

VIII.

O poet heart! O seraph soul! by men and maids
  adorèd!
O Titan with the lion's mane, and with the splendid
  forehead!
We men who bow to thee in grief must tremble in our
  gladness,
To know what tears were turned to pearls to crown thee
  in thy sadness.

IX.

An Angel by direct descent, a German by alliance,
Thou didst intone the wonder-chords which made Despair
    a science.
Yea, thou didst strike so grand a note that, in its large
    vibration,
It seemed the roaring of the sea in nature's jubilation.

X.

O Sire of Song! Sonata-King! Sublime and loving
    master;
The sweetest soul that ever struck an octave in disaster;
In thee were found the fires of thought—the splendours of
    endeavour,—
And thou shalt sway the minds of men for ever and for
    ever!

A RHAPSODY OF DEATH.

THAT phantoms fair, with radiant hair,
  May seek at midnight hour
The sons of men, belov'd again,
  And give them holy power;
That souls survive the mortal hive, and sinless come and
    go,
Is true as death, the prophet saith; and God will have
    it so.

For who be ye who doubt and prate?
  O sages! make it clear
If ye be more than men of fate,
  Or less than men of cheer;
If ye be less than bird or beast? O brothers! make it
    plain
If ye be bankrupts at a feast, or sharers in a gain.

III.

You say there is no future state;
   The clue ye fail to find.
The flesh is here, and bones appear
   When graves are undermined.
But of the soul, in time of dole, what answer can ye
    frame—
Ye who have heard no spirit-word to guide ye to the
    same.

IV.

Ah! facts are good, and reason's good,
   But fancy's stronger far;
In weal or woe we only know
   We know not what we are.
The sunset seems a raging fire, the clouds roll back,
    afraid;
The rainbow seems a broken lyre on which the storm has
    play'd.

V.

But these, ye urge, are outward signs.
   Such signs are not for you.
The sight's deceiv'd and truth bereav'd
   By diamonds of the dew.
The sage's mind is more refined, his rapture more
    complete;
He almost knows the little rose that blossoms at his
    feet!

VI.

The sage can kill a thousand things,
  And tell the names of all;
And wrench away the wearied wings
  Of eagles when they fall;
And calmly trace the lily's grace, or fell the strongest
    tree,
And almost feel, if not reveal, the secrets of the sea.

VII.

But can he set, by day or night,
  The clock-work of the skies?
Or bring the dead man back to sight
  With soul-invested eyes?
Can he describe the ways of life, the wondrous ways of
    death,
And whence it came, and what the flame that feeds the
    vital breath?

VIII.

If he could do such deeds as these,
  He might, though poor and low,
Explain the cause of Nature's laws,
  Which none shall ever know;
He might recall the vanish'd years by lifting of his
    hand,
And bid the wind go north or south to prove what he has
    plann'd.

IX.

But God is just.   He burdens not
 The shoulders of the sage;
He pities him whose sight is dim;
 He turns no second page.
There are two pages to the book.   We men have read the
   one;
The other needs a spirit-look, in lands beyond the sun.

X.

The other needs a poet's eye,
 Like that of Milton blind;
The light of Faith which cannot die,
 Though doubts perplex the mind;
The eyesight of a little child; a martyr's eye in dole,
Which sees afar the golden star that shines upon the soul!

A PRAYER FOR LIGHT.

OH, give me light, to-day, or let me die,—
  The light of love, the love-light of the sky,—
That I, at length, may see my darling's face
          One minute's space.

II.

Have I not wept to know myself so weak
That I can feel, not see, the dimpled cheek,
The lips, the eyes, the sunbeams that enfold
          Her locks of gold ?

III.

Have I not sworn that I will not be wed,
But mate my soul with hers on my death-bed ?
The soul can see,—for souls are seraphim,—
          When eyes are dim.

IV.

Oh, hush! she comes. I know her. She is nigh.
She brings me death, true heart, and I will die.
She brings me love, for love and life are one
                    Beyond the sun.

V.

This is the measure, this, of all my joys:
Life is a curse and Death's a counterpoise.
Give me thy hand, O sweet one, let me know
                    Which path I go.

VI.

I cannot die if thou be not a-near,
To lead me on to Life's appointed sphere.
O spirit-face, O angel, with thy breath
                    Kiss me to death !

MIRAGE.

'TIS a legend of a lover,
    'Tis a ballad to be sung,
In the gloaming,—under cover,—
    By a minstrel who is young;
By a singer who has passion, and who sways us with his
    tongue.

II.

I, who know it, think upon it,
    Not unhappy, tho' in tears,
And I gather in a sonnet
    All the glory of the years;
And I kiss and clasp a shadow when the substance
    disappears.

III.

Ah! I see her as she faced me,
    In the sinless summer days,
When her little hands embraced me,
    And I saddened at her gaze,
Thinking, Sweet One! will she love me when we walk in
    other ways?

IV.

Will she cling to me as kindly
    When the childish faith is lost?
Will she pray for me as blindly,
    Or but weigh the wish and cost,
Looking back on our lost Eden from the girlhood she has
    cross'd?

V.

Oh! I swear by all I honour,
    By the graves that I endow,
By the grace I set upon her,
    That I meant the early vow,—
Meant it much as men and women mean the same thing
    spoken now.

VI.

But her maiden troth is broken,
   And her mind is ill at ease,
And she sends me back no token
   From her home beyond the seas;
And I know, though nought is spoken, that she thanks me
   on her knees.

VII.

Yes, for pardon freely granted;
   For she wrong'd me, understand,
And my life is disenchanted,
   As I wander through the land
With the sorrows of dark morrows that await me in a
   band.

VIII.

Hers was sweetest of sweet faces,
   Hers the tenderest eyes of all!
In her hair she had the traces
   Of a heavenly coronal,
Bringing sunshine to sad places where the sunlight could
   not fall.

IX.

She was fairer than a vision;
  Like a vision, too, has flown.
I who flushed at her decision,
  Lo! I languish here alone;
And I tremble when I tell you that my anger was mine
  own.

X.

Not for her, sweet sainted creature.!
  Could I curse her to her face?
Could I look on form and feature,
  And deny the inner grace?
Like a little wax Madonna she was holy in the place.

XI.

And I told her, in mad fashion,
  That I loved her,—would incline
All my life to this one passion,
  And would kneel as at a shrine;
And would love her late and early, and would teach her
  to be mine.

XII.

Now in dreams alone I meet her
With my lowly human praise:
She is sweeter and completer,
And she smiles on me always;
But I dare not rise and greet her as I did in early days.

A MOTHER'S NAME.

I.

I LOVE the sound! The sweetest under Heaven,
  That name of mother,—and the proudest, too.
As babes we breathe it, and with seven times seven
  Of youthful prayers, and blessings that accrue,
We still repeat the word, with tender steven.
  Dearest of friends! dear mother! what we do
This side the grave, in purity of aim,
Is glorified at last by thy good name.

II.

But how forlorn the word, how full of woe,
  When she who bears it lies beneath the clod.
In vain the orphan child would call her so,—
  She comes not back: her place is up with God.
The wintry winds are wailing o'er the snow;
  The flowers are dead that once did grace the sod.
Ah, lose not heart! Some flowers may fade in gloom,
But Hope's a plant grows brightest on the tomb!

A SONG OF SERVITUDE.

THIS is a song of serfs that I have made,
   A song of sympathy for grief and joy:—
The old, the young, the lov'd and the betrayed,
All, all must serve, for all must be obeyed.

II.

There are no tyrants but the serving ones,
   There are no servants but the ruling men.
The Captain conquers with his army's guns,
But he himself is conquered by his sons.

III.

What is a parent but a daughter's slave,
   A son's retainer when the lad is ill?
The great Creator loves the good and brave,
And makes a flower the spokesman of a grave.

IV.

The son is servant in his father's halls,
   The daughter is her mother's maid-of-work.
The welkin wonders when the ocean calls,
And earth accepts the raindrop when it falls.

V.

There are no "ups" in life, there are no "downs,"
   For "high" and "low" are words of like degree;
He who is light of heart when Fortune frowns,
He is a king though nameless in the towns.

VI.

None is so lofty as the sage who prays,
   None so unhigh as he who will not kneel.
The breeze is servant to the summer days,
And he is bowed-to most who most obeys.

VII.

These are the maxims that I take to heart,
   Do thou accept them, reader, for thine own;
Love well thy work; be truthful in the mart,
And foes will praise thee when thy friends depart.

VIII.

None shall upbraid thee then for thine estate,
    Or show thee meaner than thou art in truth.
Make friends with death; and God who is so great,
He will assist thee to a nobler fate.

IX.

None are unfit to serve upon their knees
    The saints of prayer, unseen but quick to hear.
The flowers are servants to the pilgrim bees,
And wintry winds are tyrants of the trees.

X.

All things are good; all things incur a debt,
    And all must pay the same, or soon or late
The sun will rise betimes, but he must set;
And Man must seek the laws he would forget.

XI.

There are no mockeries in the universe,
    No false accounts, no errors that will thrive.
The work we do, the good things we rehearse,
Are boons of Nature basely named a curse.

XII.

"Give us our daily bread!" the children pray,
  And mothers plead for them while thus they speak.
But "Give us work, O God!" we men should say,
That we may gain our bread from day to day.

XIII.

'Tis not alone the crown that makes the king;
  'Tis service done, 'tis duty to his kind.
The lark that soars so high is quick to sing,
And proud to yield allegiance to the spring.

XIV.

And we who serve ourselves, whate'er befall
  Athwart the dangers of the day's behests,
Oh, let's not shirk, at joy or sorrow's call,
The service due to God who serves us all!

SYLVIA IN THE WEST.

I.

WHAT shall be done?   I cannot pray;
  And none shall know the pangs I feel.
If prayers could alter night to day,—
  Or black to white,—I might appeal;
I might attempt to sway thy heart,
And prove it mine, or claim a part.

II.

I might attempt to urge on thee
  At least the chance of some redress:—
An hour's revoke,—a moment's plea,—
  A smile to make my sorrows less.
I might indeed be taught in time
To blush for hope, as for a crime!

III.

But thou art stone, though soft and fleet,—
  A statue, not a maiden, thou!
A man may hear thy bosom beat
  When thou hast sworn some idle vow.
But not for love, no! not for this;
For thou wilt sell thy bridal kiss.

IV.

I mean, thy friends will sell thy love,
  As loves are sold in England, here.
A man will buy my golden dove,—
  I doubt he'll find his bargain dear!
He'll lose the wine; he'll buy the bowl,
The life, the limbs, but not the soul.

V.

So, take thy mate and all his wealth,
  And all the joys that wait on fame.
Thou'lt weep,—poor martyr'd one!—by stealth,
  And think of me, and shriek my name;
Yes, in his arms!   And wake, too late,
To coax and kiss the man you hate.

VI.

By slow degrees, from year to year,
   From week to week, from night to night,
He will be taught how dark and drear
   Is barter'd love,—how sad to sight
A perjured face! He will be driven
To compass Hell,—and dream of Heaven.

VII.

But stand at God's high altar there,
   With saints around thee tall and sweet,
I'll match thy pride with my despair,
   And drag thee down from glory's seat.
Yea, thou shalt kneel! Thy head shall bow
As mine is bent in anguish now.

VIII.

What! for thy sake have I forsworn
   My just ambition,—all my joy,
And all my hope from morn to morn,
   That seem'd a prize without alloy?
Have I done this? I have; and see!
I weep wild tears for thine and thee.

IX.

But I can school my soul to strength,
  And weep and wail as children do;
Be hard as stone, yet melt at length,
  And curb my pride as thou can'st, too!
But I have faith, and thou hast none;
And I have joy, but thine is done.

X.

No marriage-bells? No songs, you say?
  No flowers to grace our bridal morn?
No wine? No kiss? No wedding-day?
  I care not! Oaths are all forsworn;
And, when I clasp'd thy hand so white,
I meant to curse thee, girl, to-night.

XI.

And so I shall,—Oh! doubt not that.
  At stroke of twelve I'll curse thee twice.
When screams the owl, when swoops the bat,
  When ghosts are out I'll curse thee thrice.
And thou shalt hear!—Aye, by my troth,
One song will suit the souls of both.

XII.

I curse thy face; I curse thy hair;
  I curse thy lips that smile so well,
Thy life, thy love, and my despair,
  My loveless couch, thy wedding-bell;
My soul and thine!—Ah, see! though black,
I take one half my curses back.

XIII.

For thou and I were form'd for hate,
  For love, for scorn; no matter what.
I am thy Fere and thou my Fate,
  And fire and flood shall harm us not.
Thou shalt be kill'd and hid from ken,
And fiends will sing thy requiem then.

XIV.

Yet think not Death will serve thy stead;
  I'll find thy grave, though wall'd in stone.
I'll move thy mould to make my bed,
  And lie with thee long hours alone:—
Long, lifeless hours! Ah God, how free,
How pale, how cold, thy lips will be!

XV.

But graves are cells of truth and love,
   And men may talk no treason there.
A corpse will wear no wedding-glove,
   A ghost will make no sign in air.
But ghosts can pray? Well, let them kneel;
They, too, must loathe the love they feel.

    .   .   .   .

XVI.

Ah me! to sleep and yet to wake,
   To live so long, and yet to die;
To sing sad songs for Sylvia's sake,
   And yet no peace to gain thereby!
What have I done ?   What left unsaid ?
Nay, I will count my tears instead.

XVII.

Here is a word of wild design.
   Here is a threat; 'twas meant to warn.
Here is a fierce and freezing line,
   As hot as hate, as cold as scorn.
Ah, friend! forgive; forbear my rhymes,
But pray for me, sweet soul! sometimes.

XVIII.

Had I a curse to spare to-day,
  (Which I have not) I'd use it now.
I'd curse my hair to turn it gray,
  I'd teach my back to bend and bow;
I'd make myself so old and thin
That I should seem too sad to sin.

XIX.

And then we'd meet, we two, at night;
  And I should know what saints have known.
Thou would'st not tremble, dear, for fright,
  Or shriek to meet me there alone.
I should not then be spurned for this,
Or want a smile, or need a kiss.

XX.

I should not then be fierce as fire,
  Or mad as sin, or sharp as knife;
My heart would throb with no desire,
  For care would cool the flush of life;
And I should love thee, spotless one,
As pilgrims love some holy nun.

XXI.

Ah, queen-like creature! smile on me;
  Be kind, be good; I lov'd thee much.
I thank thee, see! on bended knee.
  I seek salvation in thy touch.
And when I sleep I watch thee come,
And both are wild, and one is dumb.

XXII.

I draw thee, ghost-like, to my heart;
  I kiss thy lips and call thee mine.
Of thy sweet soul I form a part,
  And my poor soul is part of thine.
Ah, kill me, kiss me, curse me, Thou!
But let me be thy servant now.

XXIII.

What! did I curse thy golden hair?
  Well, then, the sun will set at noon;
The face that keeps the world so fair
  Is thine, not his; he darkens soon.
Thy smile awakes the bird of dawn,
And day departs when thou art gone.

XXIV.

Oh! had I groves in some sweet star
   That shines in Heaven the whole night through,—
A steed with wings,—a golden car,—
   A something wild and strange and true:—
A fairy's wand,—an angel's crown,—
I'd merge them all in thy renown.

XXV.

I'd give thee queens to wait on thee,
   And kings to kneel to thee in prayer,
And seraph-boys by land and sea
   To do thy bidding,—earth and air
To pay thee homage,—all the flowers,—
And all the nymphs in all the bowers.

XXVI.

And this our love should last for aye,
   And we should live these thousand years.
We'd meet in Mars on Christmas Day,
   And make the tour of all the spheres.
We'd do strange things! Sweet stars would shine,
And Death would spare my love and thine.

XXVII.

But these are dreams; and dreams are vain;
    Mine most of all,—so heed them not.
Brave thoughts will die, though men complain,
    And mine was bold! 'Tis now forgot.
Well; let me bless thee, ere I sleep,
And give thee all my joys to keep.

XXVIII.

I bless the house where thou wast born,
    I bless the hours of every night,
And every hour from flush of morn
    Till death of day, for thy delight;
I bless the sunbeams as they shine,—
So like those golden locks of thine.

XXIX.

I bless thy lips, thy lustrous eyes,
    Thy face, thy feet, thy forehead fair,
The light that shines in summer skies,—
    In garden walks when thou art there,—
And all the grass beneath thy feet,
And all the songs thou singest, Sweet!

xxx.

But blessing thus,—ah, woe's the day!—
   I know what tears I shall not shed,
What flowers will bloom, and, bright as they,
   What bells will ring when I am dead.
Ah, kill me, kiss me, curse me, Thou!
But let me be thy minstrel now.

ELËANORE.

I.

THE forest flowers are faded all,
  The winds complain, the snow-flakes fall,
      Elëanore!
I turn to thee, as to a bower:—
Thou breathest beauty like a flower,
Thou smilest like a happy hour,
      Elëanore!

II.

I turn to thee.   I bless afar
Thy name, which is my guiding-star,
      Elëanore!
And yet, ah God! when thou art here
I faint, I hold my breath for fear.
Art thou some phantom wandering near,
      Elëanore?

III.

Oh, take me to thy bosom fair;
Oh, cover me with thy golden hair,
    Elëanore!
There let me lie when I am dead,
Those morning beams about me spread,
The glory of thy face o'erhead,
    Elëanore!

THE STATUE.

SEE where my lady stands,
  Lifting her lustrous hands,—
   Here let me bow.
Image of truth and grace!
Maid with the angel-face!
Earth was no dwelling-place
   For such as thou.

II.

Ah, thou unhappy stone,
Make now thy sorrows known;
   Make known thy longing.
Thou art the form of one
Whom I, with hopes undone,
Buried at set of sun,—
   All the friends thronging.

III.

Thou art some Vision bright
Lost out of Heaven at night,
　Far from thy race.
Oft when the others dance,
Come I, with wistful glance,
Fearful lest thou, perchance,
　Leave the dark place.

IV.

No! thou wilt never flee,
Earth has a charm for thee;—
　Why should we sever?
Years have I seen thee so,
Making pretence to go,
Lifting thine arms of snow,—
　Voiceless for ever!

V.

Here bring I all my cares,
Here dream and say my prayers
　While the bells toll.
O thou belovèd saint!
Let not my courage faint,
Let not not a shame, or taint,
　Injure my soul!

PABLO DE SARASATE.

WHO comes, to-day, with sunlight on his face,
 And eyes of fire, that have a sorrow's trace,
But are not sad with sadness of the years,
 Or hints of tears?

II.

He is a king, or I mistake the sign,
A king of song,—a comrade of the Nine,—
The Muses' brother, and their youngest one,
 This side the sun.

III.

See how he bends to greet his soul's desire,
His violin, which trembles like a lyre,
And seems to trust him, and to know his touch,
 Belov'd so much!

IV.

He stands full height; he draws it to his breast,
Like one, in joy, who takes a wonder-guest,—
A weird, wild thing, bewitched from end to end,—
           To be his friend.

V.

And who can doubt the right it has to lie
So near his heart, and there to sob and sigh,
And there to shake its octaves into notes
           With bird-like throats.

VI.

Ah! see how deftly, with his lifted bow,
He strikes the chords of ecstasy and woe,
And wakes the wailing of the sprite within
           That knows not sin.

VII.

A thousand heads are turn'd to where he stands,
A thousand hopes are moulded to his hands,
And, like a storm-wind hurrying from the north,
           A shout breaks forth.

VIII.

It is the welcome that of old was given
To Paganini ere he join'd in Heaven
The angel-choirs of those who serve aright
                    The God of Light.

IX.

It is the large, loud utterance of a throng
That loves a faith-employ'd, impassion'd song;
A song that soothes the heart, and makes it sad,—
                    Yet keeps us glad.

X.

For look! how bearded men and women fair
Shed tears and smile, and half repeat a prayer
And half are shamed in their so mean estate,
                    And he so great!

XI.

This is the young Endymion out of Spain
Who, laurel-crown'd, has come to us again
To re-intone the songs of other times
                    In far-off climes.

XII.

To prove again that Music, by the plea
Of all men's love, has link'd from sea to sea
All shores of earth in one serene and grand
                    Symphonic land.

XIII.

Oh! hush the while! Oh! hush! A bird has sung
A Mayday bird has trill'd without a tongue,
And now, 'twould seem, has wandered out of sight
                    For sheer delight.

XIV.

A phantom bird! 'Tis gone where all things go—
The wind, the rain, the sunshine, and the snow,
The hopes we nurs'd, the dead things lately pass'd—
                    All dreams at last.

XV.

The towers of light, the castles in the air,
The queenly things with diamonds in their hair,
The toys of sound, the flowers of magic art—
                    All these depart.

XVI.

They seem'd to live; and lo! beyond recall,
They take the sweet sad Silence for a pall,
And, wrapt therein, consent to be dismiss'd,
    Though glory-kiss'd.

XVII.

O pride of Spain! O wizard with a wand
More fraught with fervours of the life beyond
Than books have taught us in these tawdry days,
    Take thou my praise.

XVIII.

Aye, take it, Pablo! Though so poor a thing,
'Twill serve to mind thee of an English spring
When wealth, and worth, and fashion, each and all,
    Obey'd thy thrall.

XIX.

The lark that sings its love-song in the cloud
Is God-inspired and glad,—but is not proud,—
And soon forgets the salvos of the breeze,
    As thou dost these.

XX.

The shouts, the praises, and the swift acclaim,
That men have brought to magnify thy name,
Affect thee barely as an idle cheer
                Affects a seer.

XXI.

But thou art ours, O Pablo! ours to-day,
Ours, and not ours, in thy triumphant sway;
And we must urge it by the right that brings
                Honour to kings.

XXII.

Honour to thee, thou stately, thou divine
And far-famed minstrel of a mighty line!
Honour to thee, and peace, and musings high,
                Good-night! Good-bye!

MY AMAZON.

I.

MY Love is a lady fair and free,
  A lady fair from over the sea,
And she hath eyes that pierce my breast
And rob my spirit of peace and rest.

II.

A youthful warrior, warm and young,
She takes me prisoner with her tongue,
Aye! and she keeps me,—on parole,—
Till paid the ransom of my soul.

III.

I swear the foeman, arm'd for war
From *cap-à-pic*, with many a scar,
More mercy finds for prostrate foe
Than she who deals me never a blow.

IV.

And so 'twill be, this many a day;
She comes to wound, if not to slay.
But in my dreams,—in honied sleep,—
'Tis I to smile, and she to weep!

PRO PATRIA.

AN ODE TO SWINBURNE.

["We have not, alack! an ally to befriend us,
And the season is ripe to extirpate and end us.
Let the German touch hands with the Gaul,
And the fortress of England must fall.

*　　*　　*　　*　　*

Louder and louder the noise of defiance
Rings rage from the grave of a trustless alliance,
And bids us beware, and be warn'd,
As abhorr'd of all nations and scorn'd."
A Word for the Nation, by A. C. Swinburne.]

I.

NAY, good Sir Poet, read thy rhymes again,
  And curb the tumults that are born in thee,
That now thy hand, relentful, may refrain
To deal the blow that Abel had of Cain.

II.

Are we not Britons born, when all is said,
　　And thou the offspring of the knightly souls
Who fought for Charles when fears were harvested,
And Cromwell rose to power on Charles's head?

III.

O reckless, roystering bard, that in a breath
　　Did'st find the way to flout thy fathers' flag!
Is't well, unheeding what thy Reason saith,
To seem to triumph in thy country's death?

IV.

If none will speak for us, if none will say
　　How far thy muse has wrong'd us in its thought,
'Tis I will do it; I will say thee nay,
And hurl thee back the ravings of thy lay.

V.

We own thy prowess; for we've learnt by rote
　　Song after song of thine; and thou art great.
But why this malice?   Why this wanton note
Which seems to come like lava from thy throat?

VI.

When Hugo spoke we owned his master-spell;
   We knew he feared us more than he contemned.
He fleck'd with fire each sentence as it fell,
And tolled his rancours like a wedding-bell.

VII.

And we were proud of him, as France was proud.
   Ay! call'd him brother,—though he lov'd us not;
And we were thrill'd when, ruthless from a cloud,
The bolt of death outstretch'd him for a shroud.

VIII.

Thou'rt great as he by fame and force of song,
   But less than he as spokesman of his Land.
For thou hast rail'd at thine, to do it wrong,
And call'd it coward though its faith is strong.

IX.

England a coward! O thou five foot five
   Of flesh and blood and sinew and the rest!
Is she not girt with glory and alive
To hear thee buzz thy scorn of all the hive?

X.

Thou art a bee,—a bright, a golden thing
  With too much honey; and the taste thereof
Is sometimes rough, and somewhat of a sting
Dwells in the music that we hear thee sing.

XI.

Oh, thou hast wrong'd us; thou hast said of late
  More than is good for listeners to repeat.
Nay, I have marvell'd at thy words of hate,
For friends and foes alike have deem'd us great.

XII.

We are not vile. We, too, have hearts to feel;
  And not in vain have men remember'd this.
Our hands are quick at times to clasp the steel,
And strike the blows that centuries cannot heal.

XIII.

The sea-ward rocks are proud to be assail'd
  By wave and wind; for bluster kills itself,
But rocks endure. And England has prevail'd
Times out of number, when her foes have failed.

XIV.

And once, thou know'st, a giant here was found,
  Not bred in France, or elsewhere under sun.
And he was Shakespeare of the whole world round,
And he was king of men, though never crown'd.

XV.

He lov'd the gracious earth from east to west,
  And all the seas thereof and all its shores.
But most he lov'd the home that he possess'd,
And, right or wrong, his country seem'd the best.

XVI.

He was content with Albion's classic land.
  He lov'd its flag.   He veil'd its every fault.
Yes! he was proud to let its honour stand,
And bring to light the wonders it had plann'd.

XVII.

Do thou thus much; and deal no further pain;
  But sooner tear the tongue from out thy mouth,
And sooner let the life in thee be slain,
Than strike at One who strikes thee not again.

XVIII.

Thy land and mine, our England, is erect,
    And like a lordly thing she looks on thee,
And sees thee number'd with her bards elect,
And will not harm the brow that she has deck'd.

XIX.

She lets thee live.   She knows how rich and rare
    Are songs like thine, and how the smallest bird
May make much music in the summer air,
And how a curse may turn into a prayer.

XX.

Take back thy taunt, I say; and with the same
    Accept our pardon; or, if this offend,
Why then no pardon, e'en in England's name.
We have our country still, and thou thy fame!

THE LITTLE GRAVE.

I.

A LITTLE mound of earth
    Is all the land I own:
Death gave it me,—five feet by three,
    And mark'd it with a stone.

II.

My home, my garden-grave,
    Where most I long to go!
The ground is mine by right divine,
    And Heaven will have it so.

III.

For here my darling sleeps,
    Unseen,—arrayed in white,—
And o'er the grass the breezes pass,
    And stars look down at night.

IV.

Here Beauty, Love, and Joy,
   With her in silence dwell,
As Eastern slaves are thrown in graves
   Of kings remember'd well.

V.

But here let no man come,
   My mourning rights to sever.
Who lieth here is cold and dumb.
   Her dust is mine for ever!

A DIRGE.

I.

A RT thou lonely in thy tomb?
　　Art thou cold in such a gloom?
Rouse thee, then, and make me room,—
　　　　　Miserere Domine!

II.

Phantoms vex thy virgin sleep,
Nameless things around thee creep,
Yet be patient, do not weep,—
　　　　　Miserere Domine!

III.

O be faithful! O be brave!
Naught shall harm thee in thy grave;
Let the restless spirits rave,—
　　　　　Miserere Domine!

IV.

When my pilgrimage is done,
When the grace of God is won,
I will come to thee, my nun,—
Miserere Domine!

V.

Like a priest in flowing vest,
Like a pale, unbidden guest,
I will come to thee and rest,—
Miserere Domine!

DAISIES OUT AT SEA.

I.

THESE are the buds we bear beyond the surf,—
  Enshrined in mould and turf,—
To take to fields far off, a land's salute
  Of high and vast repute,—
The Shakespeare-land of every heart's desire,
Whereof, 'tis said, the fame shall not expire,
But shine in all men's thoughts as shines a beacon-fire.

II.

O bright and gracious things that seem to glow
  With frills of winter snow,
And little golden heads that know the sun,
  And seasons half begun,
How blythe they look, how fresh and debonair,
In this their prison on the seaward air,
On which no lark has soar'd to improvise a prayer.

III.

Have they no memory of the inland grass,—
  The fields where breezes pass,
And where the full-eyed children, out at play,
  Make all the land so gay?
Have they no thought of dews that, like a tear,
Were shed by Morning on the Night's cold bier,
In far-off English homes, belov'd by all men here ?

IV.

O gems of earth!   O trinkets of the spring!
  The sun, your gentle king,
Who counts your leaves and marshals ye apace,
  In many a sacred place,
The godlike summer sun will miss ye all,
For he has foster'd all things, great and small,
Yea, all good things that live on earth's revolving ball.

V.

But when, on deck, he sees with eye serene
  The kirtles, tender-green,
And fair fresh faces of his hardy flowers,
  How will he throb for hours,
And wish the lark, the laureate of the light,
Were near at hand, to see so fair a sight,
And chant the joys thereof in words we cannot write.

VI.

Oh, I have lov'd ye more than may be told,
    And deem'd it fairy-gold,—
And fairy-silver,—that ye bear withal;
    Ye are so soft and small,
I weep for joy to find ye here to-day
So near to Heaven, and yet so far away,
In our good ocean-ship, whose bows are wet with spray.

VII.

Ye are the cynosure of many eyes
    Bright-blue as English skies,—
The sailors' eyes that scan ye in a row,
    As if intent to show
That this dear freight of mould and meadow-flower
Which sails the sea, in sunshine and in shower,
Is England's gift of love, which storms shall not devour.

VIII.

She sends ye forth in sadness and in joy,
    As one may send a toy
To children's children, bred in other lands
    By love-abiding hands.
And, day by day, ye sail upon the foam
To call to mind the sires' and mothers' home,
Where babes, now grown to men, were wont of yore to
    roam.

IX.

In England's name, in Shakespeare's,—and in ours,
    Who bear these trusted flowers,—
There shall be heard a cheer from many throats,
    A rush and roar of notes,
As loud, and proud, as those of heavenward birds;
And they who till the ground and tend the herds
Will read our thoughts therein, and clothe the same in
    words.

X.

For England's sake, for England once again,
    In pride and power and pain,
For England, aye! for England in the girth
    Of all her joy and worth,
A strong and clear, outspoken, undefined,
And uncontroll'd wild shout upon the wind,
Will greet these winsome flowers as friends of human-
    kind!

Sonnets.

I.

ECSTASY.

I CANNOT sing to thee as I would sing
   If I were quickened like the holy lark
With fire from Heaven and sunlight on his wing,
   Who wakes the world with witcheries of the dark

Renewed in rapture in the reddening air.
   A thing of splendour do I deem him then,
A feather'd frenzy with an angel's throat,
A something sweet that somewhere seems to float
   'Twixt earth and sky, to be a sign to men.
He fills me with such wonder and despair!
   I long to kiss thy locks, so golden bright,
As he doth kiss the tresses of the sun.
Oh! bid me sing to thee, my chosen one,
   And do thou teach me, Love, to sing aright!

II.

VISIONS.

The Poet meets Apollo on the hill,
   And Pan and Flora and the Paphian Queen,
And infant naïads bathing in the rill,
   And dryad maids that dance upon the green,
   And fauns and Oreads in the silver sheen
They wear in summer, when the air is still.
He quaffs the wine of life, and quaffs his fill,
   And sees Creation through its mask terrene.
The dead are wise, for they alone can see
   As see the bards,—as see, beyond the dust,
   The eyes of babes.   The dead alone are just.
There is no comfort in the bitter fee
That scholars pay for fame.   True sage is he
   Who doubts all doubt, and takes the soul on trust.

III.

THE DAISY.

S<small>EE</small> where it stands, the world-appointed flower,
  Pure gold at centre, like the sun at noon,—
A mimic sun to light a true-love bower
  For fair Queen Mab, now dead or in a swoon,
  Whom late a poet saw beneath the moon.
It lifts its dainty face till sunset hour,
As if endowed with nympholeptic power,—
  Then shuts its petals like a folding tune!
I love it more than words of mine can say,
  And more than anchorite may breathe in prayer.
  Methinks the lark has made it still his care
To brag of daisies to the lord of day.
Well! I will follow suit, as best I may,
  Launching my love-songs on the summer air.

IV.

PROBATION.

Could I, O Love! obtain a charter clear
  To be thy bard, in all thy nights and days,
I would consult the stars, from year to year,
  And talk with trees, and learn of them their ways,
And why the nymphs so seldom now appear
  In human form, with rapt and earnest gaze;
  And I would learn of thee why Joy decays,
And why the Fauns have ceas'd to flourish here.

I would, in answer to the wind's " Alas!"
    Explain the causes of a sorrow's flight;
I would peruse the writing on the grass
    Which flowers have traced in blue and red and white;
And, reading these, I would, as from a pen,
Read thoughts of thine unguess'd by other men!

V.

DANTE.

HE liv'd and lov'd; he suffer'd; he was poor;
  But he was gifted with the gifts of Heaven,
  And those of all the week-days that are seven,
And those of all the centuries that endure.
He bow'd to none; he kept his honour sure.
  He follow'd in the wake of those Eleven
  Who walk'd with Christ, and lifted up his steven *
To keep the bulwarks of his faith secure.
He knew the secrets of the singing-time;
  He track'd the sun; he ate the luscious fruit
  Of grief and joy; and with his wonder-lute
He made himself a name in every clime.
  The minds of men were madly stricken mute
And all the world lay subject to his rhyme!

* Steven, a voice; old word revived.

VI.

DIFFIDENCE.

I CANNOT deck my thought in proud attire,
 Or make it fit for thee in any dress,
Or sing to thee the songs of thy desire,
In summer's heat, or by the winter's fire,
 Or give thee cause to comfort or to bless.
 For I have scann'd mine own unworthiness
And well I know the weakness of the lyre
 Which I have striven to sway to thy caress.
Yet must I quell my tears and calm the smart
 Of my vext soul, and steadfastly emerge
 From lonesome thoughts, as from the tempest's surge.
I must control the beating of my heart,
And bid false pride be gone, who, with his art,
 Has press'd, too long, a suit I dare not urge.

VII.

FAIRIES.

GLORY endures when calumny hath fled;
   And fairies show themselves, in friendly guise,
To all who hold a trust beyond the dead,
   And all who pray, albeit so worldly-wise,
   With cheerful hearts or wildly-weeping eyes.
They come and go when children are in bed
   To gladden them with dreams from out the skies
And sanctify all tears that they have shed!

Fairies are wing'd for wandering to and fro.
   They live in legends; they survive the Greeks.
Wisdom is theirs; they live for us and grow,
   Like things ambrosial, fairer than the freaks
Of signs and seasons which the poets know,
   Or fires of sunset on the mountain-peaks.

VIII.

SPIRIT LOVE.

How great my joy! How grand my recompense!
   I bow to thee; I keep thee in my sight.
I call thee mine, in love though not in sense
I share with thee the hermitage immense
   Of holy dreams which come to us at night,
When, through the medium of the spirit-lens
   We see the soul, in its primeval light,
   And Reason spares the hopes it cannot blight.
It is the soul of thee, and not the form,
   And not the face, I yearn-to in my sleep.
It is thyself.   The body is the storm,
   The soul the star beyond it in the deep
   Of Nature's calm.   And yonder on the steep
The Sun of Faith, quiescent, round, and warm!

IX.

AFTER TWO DAYS.

ANOTHER night has turned itself to day,
  Another day has melted into eve,
And lo! again I tread the measured way
    Of word and thought, the twain to interweave,
    As flowers absorb the rays that they receive.
And, all along the woodland where I stray,
I think of thee, and Nature keeps me gay,
    And sorrow soothes the soul it would bereave.
Nor will I fear that thou, so far apart,
  So dear to me, so fair, and so benign,
Wilt un-desire the fealty of a heart
    Which evermore is pledg'd to thee and thine,
And turns to thee, in regions where thou art,
    To hymn the praises of thy face divine!

X.

BYRON.

HE was a god descended from the skies
　To fight the fight of Freedom o'er a grave,
　And consecrate a hope he could not save;
For he was weak withal, and foolish-wise.
Dark were his thoughts, and strange his destinies,
　And oftentimes his life he did deprave.
But all do pity him, though none despise.
　He was a prince of song, though sorrow's slave.
He ask'd for tears,—and they were tinged with fire;
　He ask'd for love, and love was sold to him.
　He look'd for solace at the goblet's brim,
And found it not; then wept upon his lyre.
He sang the songs of all the world's desire,—
　He wears the wreath no rivalry can dim!

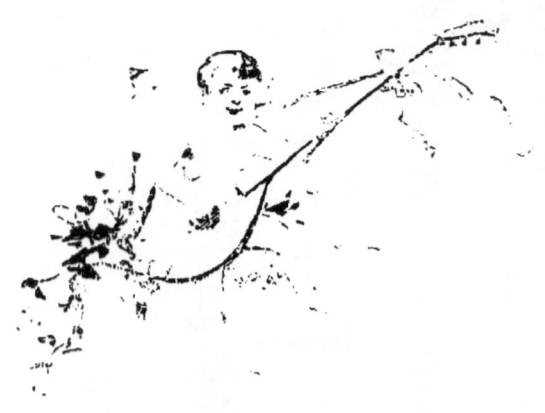

XI.

LOVE'S AMBITION.

I must invoke thee for my spirit's good,
  And prove myself un-guilty of the crime
Of mere self-seeking, though with this imbued.
I sing as sings the mavis in a wood,
  Content to be alive at harvest time.
Had I its wings I should not be withstood!
  But I will weave my fancies into rhyme,
  And greet afar the heights I cannot climb.

228

I will invoke thee, Love! though far away,
  And pay thee homage, as becomes a knight
  Who longs to keep his true-love in his sight.
Yea, I will soar to thee, in roundelay,
In shine and shower, and make a bold assay
  Of each fond hope, to compass thee aright.

XII.

LOVE'S DEFEAT.

Do what I will, I cannot chant so well
    As other men; and yet my soul is true.
My hopes are bold; my thoughts are hard to tell,
    But thou can'st read them, and accept them, too,
    Though, half-abash'd, they seem to hide from view.
I strike the lyre, I sound the hollow shell;
And why? For comfort, when my thoughts rebel,
    And when I count the woes that must ensue.
But for this reason, and no other one,
    I dare to look thy way, and bow my head
To thy sweet name, as sunflower to the sun,
    Though, peradventure, not so wisely fed
    With garden fancies. Tears must now be shed,
Unnumber'd tears, till life or love be done!

XIII.

A THUNDERSTORM AT NIGHT.

THE lightning is the shorthand of the storm
    That tells of chaos; and I read the same
    As one may read the writing of a name,—
As one in Hell may see the sudden form
    Of God's fore-finger pointed as in blame.
How weird the scene!   The Dark is sulphur-warm
With hints of death; and in their vault enorme
    The reeling stars coagulate in flame.
And now the torrents from their mountain-beds
    Roar down uncheck'd; and serpents shaped of mist
Writhe up to Heaven with unforbidden heads;
    And thunder-clouds, whose lightnings intertwist,
Rack all the sky, and tear it into shreds,
    And shake the air like Titians that have kiss'd!

XIV.

IN TUSCANY.

Dost thou remember, friend of vanish'd days,
  How in the golden land of love and song,
We met in April in the crowded ways
  Of that fair city where the soul is strong,
Aye! strong as fate, for good or evil praise?
And how the lord whom all the world obeys,—
  The lord of light to whom the stars belong,—
  Illumed the track that led thee through the throng?

Dost thou remember, in the wooded dale,
 Beyond the town of Dante the Divine,
 How all the air was flooded as with wine ?
And how the lark, to drown the nightingale,
Peal'd out sweet notes ? I live to tell the tale.
 But thou ? Oblivion signs thee with a sign !

XV.

A HERO.

The warrior knows how fitful is the fight,—
    How sad to live,—how sweet perchance to die.
Is Fame his joy ? He meets her on the height,
    And when he falls he shouts his battle-cry;
    His eyes are wet; our own will not be dry.
Nor shall we stint his praise, or our delight,
When he survives to serve his Land aright
    And make his fame the watchword of the sky.
In all our hopes his love is with us still;
    He tends our faith, he soothes us when we grieve.
    His acts are just; his word we must believe,
And none shall spurn him, though his blood they spill
To pierce the heart whose pride they cannot kill.—
    Death dies for him whose fame is his reprieve!

XVI.

REMORSE.

Go, get thee gone. I love thee not, I swear;
　And if I lov'd thee well in days gone by,
And if I kiss'd, and trifled with thy hair,
　And crown'd my love, to prove the same a lie,
　My doom is this: my joy was quick to die.
The chain of custom in the drowsy lair
Of some slain vision, is a weight to bear,
　And both abhorr'd it,—thou as well as I.
Ah, God! 'tis tearful true; and I repent;
　And like a dead, live man I live for this:—
　To stand, unvalued, on a dream's abyss,
And be my own most piteous monument.
　What! did I rob thee, Lady, of a kiss?
There, take it back; and frown; and be content!

XVII.

THE MISSION OF THE BARD.

He is a seer.   He wears the wedding-ring
   Of Art and Nature; and his voice is bold.
He should be quicker than the birds to sing,
   And fill'd with frenzy like the men of old
Who sang their songs for country and for king.
    Nothing should daunt him, though the news were told
    By fiends from Hell!   He should be swift to hold
And swift to part with truth, as from a spring.
    He should discourse of war and war's alarm,
And deeds of peace, and garlands to be sought,
    And love, and lore, and death, and beauty's charm,
And warlike men subdued by tender thought,
And grief dismiss'd, and hatred set at nought,
    And Freedom shielded by his strong right arm!

XVIII.

DEATH.

It is the joy, it is the zest of life,
  To know that Death, ungainly to the vile,
Is not a traitor with a reckless knife,
  And not a serpent with a look of guile,
  But one who greets us with a seraph's smile,—
An angel—guest to tend us after strife,
  And keep us true to God when fears are rife,
  And sceptic thought would daunt us or defile.

237

He walks the world as one empower'd to fill
  The fields of space for Father and for Son.
  He is our friend, though morbidly we shun
His tender touch,—a cure for every ill.
  He is the king of peace, when all is done.
Earth and the air are moulded to his will.

XIX.

TO ONE I LOVE.

Oh, let me plead with thee to have a nook,
  A garden nook, not far from thy domain,
That there, with harp, and voice, and poet-book,
  I may be true to thee, and, passion-fain,
  Rehearse the songs of nature once again:—
The songs of Cynthia wandering by the brook
  To soothe the raptures of a lover's pain,
And those of Phyllis with her shepherd's crook!
I die to serve thee, and for this alone,—
  To be thy bard-elect, from day to day,—
I would forego the right to fill a throne.
  I would consent to be the famine-prey
Of some fierce pard, if ere the night were flown
  I could subdue thy spirit to my sway.

XX.

EX TENEBRA.

The winds have shower'd their rains upon the sod,
   And flowers and trees have murmur'd as with lips.
The very silence has appeal'd to God.
In man's behalf, though smitten by His rod.
   'Twould seem as if the blight of some eclipse
   Had dull'd the skies,—as if, on mountain tips,
The winds of Heaven had spurn'd the life terrene,
   And clouds were foundering like benighted ships.
But what is this, exultant, unforseen,
   Which cleaves the dark ? A fearful, burning thing!
   Is it the moon ? Or Saturn's scarlet ring
Hurl'd into space ? It is the tempest-sun!
   It is the advent of the Phœban king
Which tells the valleys that the storm is done!

XXI.

VICTOR HUGO.

VICTOR the King! alive to-day, not dead!
　Behold, I bring thee with a subject's hand
　A poor pale wreath, the best at my command,
But all unfit to deck so grand a head.
　It is the outcome of a neighbour land
Denounced of thee, and spurn'd for many years.
It is the token of a nation's tears
　Which oft has joy'd in thee, and shall again.
　Love for thy hate, applause for thy disdain,—
These are the flowers we spread upon thy hearse.
We give thee back, to-day, thy poet-curse;
　We call thee friend; we ratify thy reign.
Kings change their sceptres for a funeral stone,
But thou hast turn'd thy tomb into a throne!

XXII.

CYNTHIA.

O LADY Moon, elect of all the spheres
   To be the guardian of the ocean-tides,
I charge thee, say, by all thy hopes and fears,
   And by thy face, the oracle of brides,
   Why evermore Remorse with thee abides?
Is life a bane to thee, and fraught with tears,
   That thus forlorn and sad thou dost confer

With ghosts and shades ?   Perchance thou dost aspire
To bridal honours, and thy Phœbus-sire
   Forbids the banns, whoe'er thy suitor be ?
Is this thy grievance, O thou chief of nuns ?
   Or dost thou weep to know that Jupiter
Hath many moons—his daughters and his sons—
   And Earth, thy mother, only one in thee ?

XXIII.

PHILOMEL.

Lo, as a minstrel at the court of Love,
 The nightingale, who knows his mate is nigh,
Thrills into rapture; and the stars above
 Look down, affrighted, as they would reply.
 There is contagion, and I know not why,
In all this clamour, all this fierce delight,
 As if the sunset, when the day did swoon,
 Had drawn some wild confession from the moon.
Have wrongs been done? Have crimes enacted been
To shame the weird retirement of the night?
 O clamourous bird! O sad, sweet nightingale!
Withhold thy voice, and blame not Beauty's queen.
 She may be pure, though dumb: and she is pale,
And wears a radiance on her brow serene.

XXIV.

THE SONNET KING.

O PETRARCH! I am here. I bow to thee,
   Great king of sonnets, thronèd long ago
And lover-like, as Love enjoineth me,
   And miser-like, enamoured of my woe,
   I reckon up my teardrops as they flow.
I would not lose the power to shed a tear
   For all the wealth of Plutus and his reign.
   I would not be so base as not complain
When she I love is absent from my sight.
No, not for all the marvels of the night,
   And all the varying splendours of the year.
Do thou assist me, thou! that art the light
   Of all true lovers' souls, in all the sphere,
To make a May-time of my sorrows slain.

XXV.

TOKEN FLOWERS.

Oh, not the daisy, for the love of God!
  Take not the daisy; let it bloom apace
  Untouch'd alike by splendour or disgrace
Of party feud. Its stem is not a rod;
And no one fears, or hates it, on the sod.
  It laughs, exultant, in the Morning's face,
  And everywhere doth fill a lowly place,
Though fraught with favours for the darkest clod.

'Tis said the primrose is a party flower,
  And means coercion, and the coy renown
  Of one who toil'd for country and for crown.
This may be so!   But, in my Lady's bower,
It means content,—a hope,—a golden hour.
  Primroses smile; and daisies cannot frown!

XXVI.

A PRAYER FOR ENGLAND.

Ah, fair Lord God of Heaven, to whom we call,—
  By whom we live,—on whom our hopes are built,—
  Do Thou, from year to year, e'en as Thou wilt,
Control the Realm, but suffer not to fall
Its ancient faith, its grandeur, and its thrall!
  Do Thou preserve it, in the hours of guilt,
  When foemen thirst for blood that should be spilt,
And keep it strong when traitors would appal.
Uphold us still, O God! and be the screen
  And sword and buckler of our England's might,
That foemen's wiles, and woes which intervene,
  May fade away, as fades a winter's night.
Thine ears have heard us, and Thine eyes have seen.
  Wilt Thou not help us, Lord! to find the Light?

XXVII.

A VETERAN POET.

I KNEW thee first as one may know the fame
  Of some apostle, as a man may know
  The mid-day sun far-shining o'er the snow.
I hail'd thee prince of poets ! I became
Vassal of thine, and warm'd me at the flame
  Of thy pure thought, my spirit all aglow
  With dreams of peace, and pomp, and lyric show,
And all the splendours, Master ! of thy name.
But now, a man reveal'd, a guide for men,
  I see thy face, I clasp thee by the hand ;
  And though the Muses in thy presence stand,
There's room for me to loiter in thy ken.
O lordly soul ! O wizard of the pen !
  What news from God ? What word from Fairyland ?

A CHORAL ODE TO LIBERTY.

A CHORAL ODE TO LIBERTY.

I.

O SUNLIKE Liberty, with eyes of flame,
   Mother and maid, immortal, man's delight!
Fairest and first art thou in name and fame
   And none shall rob thee of thy vested right.
Where is the man, though fifty times a king,
Shall stay the tide, or countermand the spring?
And where is he, though fifty times a knave,
Shall track thy steps to cast thee in a grave?

II.

Old as the sun art thou, and young as morn,
   And fresh as April when the breezes blow,
And girt with glory like the growing corn,
   And undefiled like mountains made of snow.
Oh, thou'rt the summer of the souls of men,
And poor men's rights, approved by sword and pen,
Are made self-certain as the day at noon,
And fair to view as flowers that grow in June.

III.

Look, where erect and tall thy Symbol waits,*
   The gift of France to friends beyond the deep,
A lofty presence at the ocean-gates
   With lips of peace and eyes that cannot weep ;
A new-born Tellus with uplifted arm
To light the seas, and keep the land from harm—
To light the coast at downfall of the day,
And dower with dawn the darkening water-way.

IV.

O sunlike Liberty, with eyes of flame,
   Mother and maid, immortal, stern of vow !
Fairest and first art thou in name and fame,
   And thou shalt wear the lightning on thy brow !

V.

Who dares condemn thee with the puny breath
   Of one poor life, O thou untouched of Fate !
Who seeks to lure thee to a felon's death,
   And thou so splendid and so love-elate ?
Who dares do this and live ? Who dares assail
Thy star-kissed forehead, pure and marble-pale;
And thou so self-possessed 'mid all the stir,
And like to Pallas born of Mulciber ?

      * Bartholdi's Statue of Liberty in New York harbour.

VI.

Oh, I've beheld the sun, at setting time,
  Peep o'er the hills as if to say good-bye ;
And I have hailed it with the sudden rhyme
  Of some new thought, full-freighted with a sigh.
And I have mused:—E'en thus may Freedom fall,
And darkness shroud it like a wintry pall,
And night o'erwhelm it, and the shades thereof
Engulf the glories born of perfect love.

VII.

But there's no fall for thee; there is no tomb;
  And none shall stab thee, none shall stay thy hand.
Thy face is fair with love's eternal bloom,
  And thou shalt have all things at thy command.
A tomb for thee ? Ay, when the sun is slain
And lamps and fires make daylight on the plain,
Then may'st thou die, O Freedom! and for thee
A tomb be found where fears and dangers be.

VIII.

O sunlike Liberty, with eyes of flame,
  Mother and maid, immortal, keen of sight !
Fairest and first art thou in name and fame,
  And thou shall tread the tempest in the night !

IX.

There shall be feasting and a sound of song
  In thy great cities; and a voice divine
Shall tell of freedom all the winter long,
  And fill the air with rapture as with wine.
The spring shall hear it, spring shall hear the sound,
And summer waft it o'er the flowerful ground;
And autumn pale shall shake her withered leaves
On festal morns and star-bespangled eves.

X.

For thou'rt the smile of Heaven when earth is dim—
  The face of God reflected in the sea—
The land's acclaim uplifted by the hymn
  Of some glad lark triumphant on the lea.
Thou art all this and more! Thou art the goal
Of earth's elected ones from pole to pole,
The lute-string's voice, the world's primeval fire,
And each man's hope, and every man's desire.

XI.

O proud and pure! O gentle and sublime!
  For thee and thine, O Freedom! O my Joy!
For thee, Celestial! on the shores of time
  A throne is built which no man shall destroy.

Thou shalt be seen for miles and miles around
And wield a sceptre, though of none be crowned.
The waves shall know thee, and the winds of Heaven
Shall sing thee songs with mixed and mighty steven.

XII.

O sunlike Liberty, with eyes of flame,
 Mother and maid, immortal, unconfined!
Fairest and first art thou in name and fame,
 And thou shalt speed more swiftly than the wind!

XIII.

Who loves thee not is traitor to himself,
 Traitor is he to God and to the grave,
Poor as a miser with his load of pelf,
 And more unstable than a leeward wave.
Cursèd is he for aye, and his shall be
A name of shame from sea to furthest sea,
A name of scorn to all men under sun
Whose upright souls have learnt to loathe this one.

XIV.

A thousand times, O Freedom! have I turned
 To thy rapt face, and wished that martyr-wise
I might achieve some glory, such as burned
 Within the depths of Gordon's azure eyes.

Ah God! how sweet it were to give thee life,
To aid thy cause, self-sinking in the strife,
Loving thee best, O Freedom! and in tears
Giving thee thanks for death-accepted years.

XV.

For thou art fearful, though so grand of soul,
    Fearful and fearless and the friend of men.
The haughtiest kings shall bow to thy control,
    And rich and poor shall take thy guidance then.
Who doubts the daylight when he sees afar
The fading lamp of some night-weary star,
Which prophet-like, has heard amid the dark
The first faint prelude of the nested lark?

XVI.

O sunlike Liberty, with eyes of flame,
    Mother and maid, immortal, prompt of thought!
Fairest and first art thou in name and fame,
    And thou shalt lash the storm till it be nought!

XVII.

O thou desired of men!   O thou supreme
    And true-toned spirit whom the bards revere!
At times thou com'st in likeness of a dream
    To urge rebellion, with a face austere;

And by that power thou hast—e'en by that power
Which is the outcome of thy sovereign-dower—
Thou teachest slaves, down-trodden, how to stand
Lords of themselves in each chivalrous Land.

XVIII.

The hosts of death, the squadrons of the law,
    The arm'd appeal to pageantry and hate,
Shall serve, a space, to keep thy name in awe,
    And then collapse, as old and out of date.
Yea! this shall be; for God has willed it so.
And none shall touch thy flag, to lay it low ;
And none shall rend thy robe, that is to thee
As dawn to day, as sunlight to the sea.

XIX.

For love of thee, thou grand, thou gracious thing!
    For love of thee all seas, and every shore,
And all domains whereof the poets sing,
    Shall merge in Man's requirements evermore.
And there shall be, full soon, from north to south,
From east to west, by Wisdom's word of mouth

One code of laws that all shall understand,
And all the world shall be one Fatherland.

XX.

O sunlike Liberty, with eyes of flame,
  Mother and maid, immortal, sweet of breath !
Fairest and first art thou in name and fame,
  And thou shalt pluck Redemption out of Death !

Italian Poems

BY ERIC MACKAY

LA ZINGARELLA.
IL PONTE D'AVIGLIO.
I MIEI SALUTI.

LA ZINGARELLA.

DIMMI, dimmi, o trovatore,
    Tu che canti sul lïuto,
Bello e bruno e pien d'amore
Dalla valle in su venuto,
Non ti fermi sull' altura
Per mostrar la tua bravura?
Non mi canti sul burrone
Qualche lieta tua canzone?

— Zingarella, in sulla sera
    Canta bene il rosignolo,
Piange e canta in sua preghiera
Salutando un dolce suolo.
Ma il lïuto al mio toccare
Pianger sa, non sa pregare . . .
Deh! che vuoi col tuo sorriso,
Tu che sai di paradiso?

III.

— Vò sentire in tuo linguaggio
   Come è fatto un uom fedele,
   Se l'amor lo fa selvaggio,
   Se il destin lo fa crudele.
   Parla schietto; son profana
   Ma ben leggo l'alma umana.
   Parla pur dei tuoi vïaggi
   Nei deserti e nei villaggi.

IV.

— Canterotti, o zingarella,
   Qualche allegra mia ballata,
   Qualche estatica novella
   D' una dama innamorata . . .
   — Dimmi tutto!—Canterotti
   D' Ungheria le meste notti.
   D' Ungheria?—Del Bosco Santo
   Dove nacque il gran Sorranto.

V.

Sappi in breve, son marchese
   Castellano e cantatore,
   Cattivai con questo arnese
   D'una maga un dì l'amore.

— D' una maga?—Sì, di quelle
Che san legger nelle stelle.
— E fu bella?—Non v' è guari
Dama, oh no, che le sia pari.

VI.

Come parca in fra le dita
    Essa tenne il mio destino,
    Fu la sfinge di mia vita
    Col sorriso suo divino.
    Avea biondi i suoi capelli,
    Occhi neri e molto belli,
    Braccia e collo in puritade
    Come neve quando cade.

VII.

— Taci, taci, o castellano;
    Qui convien pregar per essa.
    — Io l'amai d'amor sovrano!
    Pronta fu la sua promessa.
    L' aspettai; mi fu cortese,
    Ma fuggì dal mio paese,
    Travestita un dì di Maggio
    Come biondo e giovin paggio.

VIII.

Oh, giammai non fu sognata
   Cosa uguale per bellezza
   Chi la vide incoronata
   Sorridea per tenerezza.
   Chi la vide di mattina
   La credeva una regina,
   Qualche sogno di poeta,
   Qualche incanto di profeta!

IX.

— Traditor! col tuo liuto
   Tu l' hai fatto innamorare!
   — Io giurai per San Bernuto
   E pel Cristo in sull' altare,
   Per Giuseppe e per Maria
   Che farei la vita pia.
   — E il facesti? — I sacri voti
   Ricantai dei sacredoti.

X.

— Or m'ascolta, o trovatore,
   Or rispondi, e dimmi il vero:
   Hai veduto il mesto fiore
   Che si coglie in cimitero?

Hai veduto i fior di rose
Che s'intreccian per le spose,
Quando cantan desolati
Gli usignoli abbandonati ?

XI.

Crolli il capo; impallidisci;
  Stendi a me la bianca mano;
Non rispondi; e forse ambisci
Della sposa ormai l'arcano?
Qui morì la Gilda, maga
Sotto il nome di Menzaga;
Quì morì, nel suo pallore,
Per l' amor d'un trovatore!

. . . .

XII.

Stravolto l' amante s'inchina;
  Ei mira la mesta donzella.
  Velata è la maga, ma bella,
Coll' occhio che pianger non sa.
      — O donna, l'amor t' indovina ...
  Tu, Gilda, t' ascondi colà!

XIII.

Nel mondo non v'è la sembianza
    Di tale e di tanta beltade!
    Non cresce per queste contrade
Nè giglio nè spirto d'amor.
    Tu sola tu sei la Speranza
    Che tenni qua stretta sul cor.

XIV.

Tu sola tu sei la mia dama,
    La gioja e l'onor della vita;
    Tu sola, donzella romita,
Del mondo la diva sei tu.
    L'amor ti conosce, e la fama;
    Nè manca l'antica virtù.

XV.

Ma dove è la fè del passato
    Che tanto brillò nella festa?
    L'amore, l'onore, le gesta
D'un tempo che presto fuggì?
    Fu vero?   L'ho forse sognato?
    Tu pur l'hai sognato così!

XVI.

La maga intenta ascolta il suo galante;
    Ride, si scioglie il velo e guarda il Sire.
    Rossa diventa e bianca in uno istante,
    E poi s' asconde il viso e vuol fuggire.
    Corre nei bracci suoi lo fido amante;
    E favellar vorria nel suo gioïre...

XVII.

— Deh! taci, oh taci! Al mondo ovunque è doglia.
    Gilda son io. Ti bacio e son contenta.
    Pianger non so se non per pazza voglia
Come la strega allor che si lamenta . . .

XVIII.

Cosa vuoi tu ? Che vuoi che sì mi guardi ?
    Diva non son, ma donna; e fui crudele.
    — Baciami in bocca. O Dio! mi stringi ed ardi
Tanto d' amore e piangi e sei fedele ?

XIX.

— Ugo! M' ascolta, io son la tua meschina,
    Forte ben sì, ma doma in questi agoni;
    Sono la schiava tua, la tua regina,
Quel che tu vuoi purché non m'abbandoni!

xx.

— O cara, o casta, o bella, o tu che braino,
   Dammi la morte unita a un tuo sorriso.
   Eva sarai per me.   Son io l'Adamo;
E quivi in terra avrassi il paradiso!

IL PONTE D'AVIGLIO.

I.

O MESTO bambino col capo chinato,
  Rispondi; rispondi. Che fece Renato?
Fu vinto Morello? Fu salvo Lindoro?
Rispondi; rispondi!—Son padre di loro.

II.

  Non veggo tornare dal Ponte d'Aviglio
Renato superbo del vinto periglio.
·L' han forse promosso? Risorge la guerra?
Rispondi; rispondi!—L' han messo sotterra.

III.

  O ciel! tu lo senti, tu vedi l'oltraggio;
Renato fu prence del nostro villaggio! . . .
Ma dimmi, piccino. Che fece Morello?
Rispondi; rispondi! — Lo chiude l' avello.

IV.

Ahi, crudo destino! Si grande, si forte,
Morello nasceva per vincer la morte.
Ma l' altro? Che fece sul campo serrato?
Rispondi; rispondi! — Morì da soldato.

V.

Gran Dio! che mi narri! Pur desso m' é tolto?
Renato m' é morto? Morello sepolto?
E piangi, . . . tu pure? Gentile bambino!
Che dici? Rispondi! — Vi resta Giannino.

VI.

Oh si, del figliuolo l'ignoto tesoro,
L' incognito figlio del biondo Lindoro.
Ma dove trovarlo nel nome di Dio?
Rispondi; rispondi! — Buon padre, son io.

I MIEI SALUTI.

I.

TI saluto, Margherita
    Fior di vita, . . . ti saluto!
    Sei la speme del mattino,
    Sei la gioja del giardino.

II.

Ti saluto, Rosignolo
    Nel tuo duolo, . . . ti saluto!
    Sei l' amante della rosa
    Che morendo si fa sposa.

III.

Ti saluto, Sol di Maggio
    Col tuo raggio, . . . ti saluto!
    Sei l' Apollo del passato,
    Sei l' amore incoronato.

IV.

Ti saluto, Donna mia,
    Casta e pia, . . . ti saluto!
    Sei la diva dei desiri,
    Sei la Santa dei Sospiri.

www.ingramcontent.com/pod-product-compliance
Lightning Source LLC
Chambersburg PA
CBHW031343070726
47496CB00017B/1491